Take This

Jan 2016

Take This

A Novel

To my best friend Jill

Steven Lewis

Happy reading!
Steve Lewis

▲ **Codhill Press**
CODHILL

New Paltz, New York

CODHILL

Codhill Press books
are published for David Appelbaum

First Edition
Printed in the United States of America
Copyright © 2015 by Steven Lewis

Cover and text design by Alicia Fox

Library of Congress Cataloging-in-Publication Data

Lewis, Steven M.
  Take this : a novel / by Steven Lewis. — First edition.
    pages ; cm
  ISBN 1-930337-86-8 (acid-free paper)
  I. Title.
  PS3612.E9855T35 2015

813'.6—dc23

2015020194

"Bob Marley isn't my name. I don't even know my name yet."

To Patti, still the one. No one else. Ever.

Acknowledgments

A lifetime of appreciation to the late poet James Hazard, mentor and dear friend, who more than 40 years ago gave me a nifty flashlight to navigate my way through the self-reflective shadows and into what I now understand is the illuminating voice.

Closer in time to this project, a deep debt of gratitude to the merry band of writers and friends from my Duckdog Cottage Retreats, each of whom has lent a voice of heartening encouragement and clear direction to this project: Cathy Allman, Stephanie Benedetto, Mary Catherine Bolster, Julie Evans, Joanna FitzPatrick, John Gredler, Mihai Grunfeld, Ed McCann, Tom Nolan, Helise Winters, Larry Winters.

Immeasurable thanks to Elizabeth Langosy, Editor Emeritus of Talking Writing, whose sensitive and rigorous and spot on editing brought this manuscript into its final form.

An enormous grateful IOU to Julie (again), Joanna (again), and Ed (again) for the tedious job of proofing the final ms.

And much closer to home, a vast and humbling hallelujah for my sixteen grandchildren, my seven children and their spouses, each of whom in the space of a hug lets me know that I am beloved.

To my wife Patricia, who stands by me, who knows me in ways no one else ever will...and still loves me.

Chapter One

Marion was standing on the front porch, waiting on the other side of the aluminum storm door.

Robert glared at her through the glass for a few moments, then pushed it open part way. She held the door open with an elbow, reached into her coat pocket and extended her free hand, a one-carat diamond solitaire engagement ring in the criss-crossed cup of her soft palm. "Robert, take this," she said.

With those winter-red cheeks and the bright morning sun behind her long, frizzy blond hair, Robert thought his ex-wife looked more like a college girl than the fifty-eight-year-old mother of his grown children. "Marion, I don't want it."

"I'm asking you, Robert—it's the only thing, the last thing, I'm asking of you. Please take it from me." Her small hand was shaking. "It belongs to you, to your family. I don't have rights to it anymore."

"I don't want anything from you."

Wide-eyed, she pushed her open palm closer to his chest.

Robert leaned heavily against the doorjamb. He shook his head. "If I take it, Marion, will you please just go?"

Her eyes pooled. "I will."

So Dr. Robert Tevis, psychotherapist, reached across the doorway and, without touching the soft skin he could still sometimes feel on his cheek, plucked his late mother's engagement ring from his ex-wife's hand and slowly closed his swollen fist around it.

"Thank you, Robert." Her blue eyes closed now. She started to say something— "I only wish you—" but then stopped. "Thank you."

He nodded, sliding his hand deep into his pocket, releasing the ring. He looked at the bare, overgrown azalea bushes at the corners of the porch, the thin coating of snow. "So…?"

Tears now flowed down her high cheeks. "I'm sorry, Robert, I'm so sorry that it all came to this. I hope—"

"Don't," he said, holding up an index finger as if warning one of the kids. "Just don't."

"Well, I—"

"Well, please don't," he said, more softly this time. Robert wanted to say what he'd rehearsed after receiving her phone call the night before: *I harbor no malice toward you, Marion. Things happen. Neither one of us is more responsible than the other. We had many good years together. I'm sure there'll come a time….* But what he said was: "Is that all?"

She nodded, then reached across the threshold to place her empty hand on his unshaven cheek. He froze, couldn't pull himself away, her cool palm soothing his burning face.

And a few moments later—after Marion had turned away, walked down the snowy path, and reached her idling car— Robert was still standing in the open doorway. "Marion," he called out.

She looked back.

"I'm sorry, too."

She shook her head, got in the car, and drove off.

A few days later, Robert's son Sam Tevis, 33, with an expanding 40-inch waist, stood in the hallway of the home he grew up in, staring at a living room empty of all but a pile of cartons, with the couch, chairs, and rug already at Goodwill and the wrought-iron fireplace set and round log holder now in his own house in the village. "Are you sure you want to do this, Dad?"

Robert smiled, reached up and laid a reassuring hand on his son's shoulder. "I am, Sam. Sam I am."

"You know you're more than welcome to stay with us—for as long as you want. " Sam's upper lip quivered. "It just doesn't seem the right time to go on the road, Dad. I mean, with your health and all…. Where are you heading?" He looked away. "And when are you coming home again?"

Robert glanced out the narrow window on one side of the door and then back at his son, now a grown man with a receding hairline, taller and more bearish than his father, already carrying a paunch, a husband, a father, the new high school vice-principal. "Well, first I'm going to see Beryl. Then, I don't know. I've got some serious thinking to do, and, I don't know, I have to try to set things right."

"But you're not healthy, Dad." Sam's lip was quivering again. "You've been through a lot. Why don't you just wait until spring?"

Robert looked back out the window. "Is Alyssa coming?"

"She's still having a hard time, you know. I don't know if she'll make it out here."

Just then, a silver BMW slid soundlessly into the snowy drive. The two men, both in red plaid flannel shirts, stood shoulder to shoulder, looking through the sidelight window as Alyssa got out, opened the back car door, and hoisted eighteen-month-old Haley, wearing a pink snowsuit, onto her hip.

"Sorry I'm late," she said from the porch, as Robert held the storm door open. "I had to drop Travis off at nursery school and stop at Rennebohm's, you know the drill."

"I'm glad you came, sweetheart."

She was on her knee, unzipping the snowsuit, when she glanced up. "Did I have a choice?"

He reached down and touched his daughter's shoulder. "I guess if there's anything to be learned from all this, it's that we all have choices."

Sam frowned, turned his back, and walked into the emptied, swept, and mopped kitchen.

"Well, if I had a choice, I wouldn't be here, Dad. You'd be right where you're supposed to be—at your goddamn office in town, listening to suburban women whining about their infantile, money-making husbands—not heading off on some ridiculous hippie-dippie adolescent road trip to find yourself. " She looked over at Sam who nodded in agreement. "And my dear sainted mother would be at my house, sitting in the kitchen, sharing a cup of coffee with me, holding this beautiful baby girl in her lap, not off in Central America fucking our motherfucking pastor."

Robert blanched. "That was harsh, Alyssa."

She raised her eyebrows. "Am I wrong? Am I wrong?"

He stood mute, hands at his side.

Her voice wavered now. "Dad, you're too old to—and you're sick. I mean, what the hell do you think you're doing, leaving like this? There's still time to patch things up with Mom, you know. The babies are—"

"Al," Sam interrupted from the kitchen, invoking the last vestiges of the Tevis children's pecking order, "I already went through all this with him. He's going. Let's just hear what he brought us here to say."

"What? What is there left to say? Frankly, I think it's all been said. Here—" She picked up the smiling baby under the armpits and thrust her toward her father. "I mean, what the hell are we doing here?"

Robert took Haley, turned her to face him, and placed her on his hip. He lowered his nose to her sweet hair and inhaled her baby scent. "I have a couple of things to give you two before I take off."

"Yeah, and where is Beryl?" Alyssa sniped. "Why the hell does she get to miss all this goodhearted family fun?"

Robert lifted his lips from the baby's soft hair. "Do I really have to explain that to you as well?"

A tear rolled down Alyssa's cheek. She shook her head. "No, I guess not," her voice barely above a whisper. "But what happened? I mean, what happened here? Sam, I do know we've been all through this, but I thought we were actually happy—or at least happy enough—in this family."

"You know…things happen, Alyssa. We *were* happy. You know that. And I hope you know that I harbor no malice toward your mother; things just happen. Neither one of us is more responsible than the other. You should know that we had many good years together." He shifted the baby to the other hip, nauseated by the clinical words coming out of his mouth, words that had been meant for Marion.

She sneered, "Thirty-four, Dad."

He nodded. "Yes, thirty-four it was," he pursed his lips, "but, well…let's say we had a good run, thirty-two or so." He looked up at the ceiling. "Thirty-one, thirty-two years for which I am eternally grateful. And I'm sure there will come a time when…." He drifted off.

"So what's up?" Sam now filled the kitchen doorway, one hand high up on each side of the trim.

"Let's sit." Robert was going to suggest sitting down at the kitchen table, but of course that was gone. He handed Haley back to her mother and walked around to the stairs and lowered himself down on the third step, his breathing now labored. "I need to sit."

Alyssa, 31, dark-haired and the kind of trim edging up on hard, waited while her father collected himself and then, glaring at her brother, could wait no longer. "Well?"

"Well, first I want to tell you something." He looked up, his eyes pooling now. "I want to tell you that I've made a mess of things." He closed his eyes. "I want to apologize—"

Sam shook his head. "You have nothing to apologize for, Dad." He looked at Alyssa who closed her eyes and shook her head like she was disgusted with the whole thing.

"Well," Robert nodding, "I do have some things to apologize for, Sam, if you'll hear me out. Maybe a lot of things. And then I want to give you each something before I take off."

"Should we sit?" Sam asked, now in the hall.

Robert shrugged. "I guess. What I'm about to tell you will not be easy to hear."

Alyssa, who once taught yoga before the kids were born, sank effortlessly to the pine floor, cross-legged and straight-backed, the baby in her lap. Sam leaned against the wall and slid down heavily, knees up.

As he'd been doing since they were little children sitting around the kitchen table, Robert waited until they were both looking at him. "There are things you need to know." He looked from one grown child to the other, still able to see the toddlers they were. "And you should know that I'm not going to sugarcoat anything, just tell you straight on." Alyssa took in a deep breath and let it out slowly. "And I'm not going to berate your mother here or beg your indulgence for my failures, I'm just going to tell you something I haven't shared before."

"Jesus Christ, Dad," Sam muttered, "just say what you to have say!"

Alyssa shot a glance over at her usually temperate brother. "Right," she said as softly as if she was speaking to her own children, "please just tell us what we need to know, what we likely already know."

Sam shot a glance over to his sister, but Robert held his hand up like a traffic cop and they both grew stony.

Robert's barrel chest rose and fell. "Well, here it is…in ninety-four and a bit into ninety-five, I was seeing a client, a woman in town, about some serious marital problems and…well, after a few months of intensive therapy where we saw each other quite regularly, one thing led to another and we had a brief affair."

Both of his grown children lifted their chins and tilted their heads ever so slightly. He let the confession sink in for a few seconds. "Before you say anything, I promise you here and now, I swear on my mother's soul that it was the only time that I cheated on your mother."

He waited now until he found Alyssa's eyes and nodded. Then did the same with Sam. "It was short-lived—a few months of stolen lust that looked like love—and, as you might imagine, it ended badly…very badly…so badly, in fact, that the woman wrote a five-page letter to your mother detailing the whole affair in excruciating detail," he bit down on his lower lip, "including where and what we did. Said some pretty harsh things," glancing again toward Alyssa who was vacantly nodding her head.

So Robert was startled for the second time that morning when Sam, not Alyssa, snorted from the periphery, "Just how the hell could you do that, Dad? I mean—"

"How do we do anything, Sam?" Robert shot back at his oldest, his only son, sitting like some overgrown boy in the corner, instantly sorry, as he always was, every time he snapped at the boy for challenging him. Only this time the boy's head was not bent down into his chest. He was glaring right back at him.

"Well, there are some things we don't do, Dad. You told me that. You goddamn told me that when I got married."

Robert buried his face in his hands. "I'm sorry, Sam." He turned to Alyssa. "I'm sorry, sweet girl. I don't know what to tell you. I am truly sorry I let you down." He was sobbing now.

The two grown children could hardly breathe. They had never seen their father, always so in command, so undone.

But Sam couldn't let go, the first time he had the old man on the ropes. He batted his hand through the breathless air at his hapless father, his voice an octave or two below a growl. "You goddamn let her down, not me. Not me, Dad. I mean, just how the fuck…?" He turned then to his sister, full of fury. "Did you know this? Did you know this?"

Alyssa nodded. Looked at her father then back at her brother, her voice just above a high-school whisper. "Not then. Last year. Two summers ago down at the beach when Beryl was deciding whether to go to Milwaukee with Stephen or stay in Asheville. "

The blood had drained out of Robert's face. "What did she say?" he asked.

"What the hell do you think Mom said?" The whisper was gone: "Y'know, you talk to me about Travis and his bed-wetting like you're such a goddamn expert on child-rearing. Why the hell are you so damn clueless about what's happening with Beryl?"

Sam's clean-shaven face looked like it was on the edge of crumbling. "What the hell did she say?"

"I don't know, she was drunk, feeling sorry for herself about not being some kind of Jane Goodall look-alike. She said she had a kind of 'revelation' after Dad broke his vows…of course, she never mentioned the salient fact that she was boinking Pastor Jeddy at the time," pausing to add with a smirk, "who apparently is not gay."

"And you didn't tell me?" asked Sam.

She shook her head.

"Why not?"

"Mom asked me not to. She was humiliated by the whole thing and didn't want anyone else to know."

Robert sat up straight, eyebrows knitted. "Is that why Beryl wouldn't speak to me?"

She nodded. "I guess."

"Oh," he said. "Oh...."

Sam glared at his sister and then shook his big head. "I don't know any of you anymore." Then he turned to his father. "So why are you telling us this crap now? Just relieving your guilt?"

"No, son...," he looked away, out the sidelight window, "I've just been thinking what a mess I've made of my life...how I hurt everyone I loved and, I don't know, I thought I owed you the truth about our marriage...so that you two wouldn't be so angry about your mother. So you'd understand how these things happen. So you'd know that things were slipping away from us years before all this with the pastor. So that I—"

Sam stood up. "I'm going."

"No, please, Sam...I have something for you."

"What?"

Robert had to squelch his standard reply, the one taken right off his list of Tough Love virtues: "Don't take that tone of voice with me. I'm your father." This time he accepted the slap for what it was. This time, inside a cold empty house, he said only, "I just wanted you to know that I bear a large measure of responsibility for leading her to the affair. That you shouldn't be mad at her. That I alone—"

"Thanks," Sam grabbed his jacket. "Now I'm going."

"No, no, no, no, wait...like I said, I have something for you. For both of you." He stood up and slid his hand in the pocket of his khakis. He held out his thick palm, two rings, one leaning on the other just below the yellowed calluses. His hand was shaking.

"Your hand is swollen, Dad, what—"

"It's nothing, nothing new, same fluid retention thing I've been dealing with for the last few years."

Alyssa looked down. "Well, I don't want Mom's frickin' ring," Her upper lip was trembling.

"But it's not Mom's—"

Sam cut in, "And I got my own, thanks." He held up his left hand and twisted the band with the fingers of his right hand.

"You know, you two might cut me a little slack here. This isn't easy, you know—"

"Well, try it from this side for once in your life!" Sam slid an arm into his down jacket.

Robert wiped some spittle from his lip. "You know," he started and then pressed his lips together. "I guess I deserved that."

Sam stood there glaring at his father.

Robert grew dizzy then and sat back down on the steps. "You know, you two could be just a goddamn tad more mature about all this—you know, it didn't happen to you. I'm the one that's all alone. So…"

"So?"

"So please take the rings, both of you." He took a step toward Sam. "Your mother loved me with all her heart when she slipped this band on my finger. Take it, please. Please. Save it for Aaron, if he should ever want it."

Chewing on his lower lip, Sam nodded like the little boy he once was, inhaled deeply, and took the ring from his father. Closed his fist around it and buried it in his pocket.

"Please tell him—" Robert began.

"Don't!" Sam held up his palm like he was directing traffic, like his father had done to him a million times.

"But I just—"

"Just don't, Dad. I will save it for him—and he'll get it in my own good time—in my own words."

Then Robert turned to Alyssa. "And you should know that I worshipped the ground your mother walked on when I slipped this ring on her finger. I adored her, heart and soul."

Alyssa closed her eyes and shook her head. "What about Beryl? What does she get?"

"I have something for her. When I drive the camper down to Asheville I'll give it to her then."

"What?"

He waved his empty hand. "It doesn't really matter, does it? I just want each of you to have something of our love. To know that your mother and I once loved each other with all our hearts."

"Well, right now, Dad, that's not nearly enough. I want...," but she couldn't go on. "I just don't want her damn ring."

"But it's not hers, Alyssa. It's not hers. It was Grandma's—she gave it to us before we got married. Mom gave it back to me a few days ago. She thought it should stay in our family."

"But—" she said, but had nowhere to go beyond that.

So, as he often did, Robert filled in the blanks, "But nothing... Haley would want it. Haley would treasure it. Please, here, take it."

Alyssa looked down at her father's swollen hand and then up at his wet eyes. "For Haley," she said. And when he did not turn away, "Not for you."

"Yes, yes, sweetheart, take this for Haley. For Haley. No one else. No one else. Take this...."

Chapter Two

The small Winnebago that Dr. Tevis bought at Camper's World on Route 213 in High Falls was not small, just smaller than the RV monsters that dwarfed it on the lot. But it was roadworthy and certainly big enough for a sixty-year-old man out for what he figured was arguably the final ride of his life.

In the back of the camper the "dining room" table folded down into a queen- size bed. Up front, right behind the driver's captain's chair, was a tiny kitchen, with a two-burner propane stove and half refrigerator. And right next to that was the tinier bathroom/shower combo that Robert, six feet two and two hundred thirty pounds, barely fit into. Just enough. And in some ways more than enough.

Robert was anxious to finally be on the road. After the gut-wrenching good-byes with Alyssa and Sam, Robert had watched his two oldest children disappear in separate cars around the bend of the snowy driveway, then he picked up the big duffel bag, the backpack, and the laptop case he'd left on the porch, carried them down the flagstone path, and dumped them through the side door of the camper.

Remembering Johnny Alesandro, who was supposed to come by and pick up the cartons of books he had donated to the Elting Library, Robert scowled and walked back to the porch one more time. He left a scribbled note on the door, turned around and scanned the once embraceable front yard where he and Marion had raised their three children. Then trudged down the snowy path to the gleaming Winnebago.

On the way through the village of Elting, Robert passed

Prospect Street and, despite urging himself onward up Main Street toward the Thruway, took a left on Grove, and circled back to his friend Garrison's house.

Garrison was up on the porch roof, shoveling snow. He held up the shovel. "So hotshot, betchyer glad you won't have to do this shit anymore."

Robert squinted up into the harsh sunlight bouncing off the snow, "There are some consolations to a life blown to pieces, Garrison." He forced a thin smile.

"Right," Garrison called back. "You should be as happy as a kid going off to college to finally get himself laid." A moment later Garrison was on his hands and knees, backing down to the ladder and then slowly, carefully lowering himself step-by-step to his old friend. "Y'know, Bob, there are probably still some people in this town who would buy that pile of shit you're selling, but not me. I'm not worried about you, buddy boy."

Robert smiled and shrugged. "I'll be okay. One thing for sure, I've been around here too long."

"I'm not buying that one either, old pal." He clapped the snow off his gloves. "But I didn't buy that piece of Disney shit you're driving either."

The two men glanced in unison at the clunky van in the driveway. Then Robert swiped at the foot of snow on the yew bushes, the bent branches springing to life with a spray of powder. "It's complicated, Garrison. This is no pleasure ride. And, you know, I still have to face Beryl and…make some big decisions."

"Sounds to me like you already made them."

Robert nodded. "I am sixty goddamn years old, my friend, all alone in the universe, and pretty much as dumb as the day I was born. I have fucked up everything."

Garrison lifted and turned the ladder so he could carry it over to the garage. "Yeah, so? You think you're alone in that?"

Robert picked up the snow shovel and followed him into the garage where, as boys forty-five years ago, they smoked cigarettes, drank beer, and salivated over *Playboy*s stolen from the top rack at Archie's barbershop on Main Street. "You're not going to cut me a break, are you?"

"Why the hell should I? You're fucking running away. Doing what you always counseled me against—don't you tell me about complicated." He tilted his head back toward the house.

"It is complicated. I've still got a lot to figure out—and I don't think I can do it around here. Too many ghosts. Too much static."

"What the hell is there to figure out?"

Robert followed him as he hung the ladder on the hooks along the south wall. "Well, for one, how I got to this pathetic point in my life."

"Gentlemen, start your violins." The smirk on Garrison's face was hard to read, though Robert knew he was about to get some advice. He waited, hands in his coat pockets. "Y'know, you should have stayed an English major with me way back when—you wouldn't have so many delusions about figuring things out—and that ridiculous affair wouldn't have involved your cold mother or your distant father. It would've just been a romp with a sexy graduate student who was just using your aged, disheveled, lumpy body for a good grade."

By then they were back on the front porch, shuffling their feet like the teenage boys they once were, one waiting for the other to call the next move. "Well," said Garrison, "I'd invite you in, but Louise is with the home health care aide…and you might scare the shit out of them with that faux Carhartt huntin' jacket you're wearing, not to mention that five-day growth of beard." He held out his arms. "You gonna be the hippie you never were?"

The two men hugged each other, stepped back and, caught in that oddly familiar male moment of not knowing what would come next, Garrison took off his old Yankees hat, tossed it on the bench, reached down into the neck of his undershirt and carefully lifted out a silver chain and pendant over his long, unruly silver hair. "Here...take this."

Robert laughed out loud like he hadn't laughed out loud in months. "You still have that thing?" That thing being a silver design with the letters S-H-I-T laid out on top of each other so that the word itself was obscured.

"Just found it in an old shoebox. Cleaning out all that accumulated junk from my misspent youth." He smiled. "I was looking for a Polaroid of us from the Wisconsin days that I wanted to give to you. Didn't find the damn picture, but then there was this, all tangled in the corner. So yeah, here, do me a big favor and take this off my hands."

Robert shook his head in amazement. "Oh, man...I have no idea what happened to mine. Remember when we—?"

Eyes down. "Yes, I do."

"I can't," Robert said, holding up the thick hand like he was stopping traffic, eyes wet.

"No?"

"No. I'm letting go of everything. Not taking on anything. You know what I mean, right?"

Garrison scowled, "Just friggin' take it, Bob. I want you to have it. There is no one else in the world who is patently immature enough to get any enjoyment out of looking at it. Maybe it'll be a lucky charm for you. Besides, it'll help even the score. So take it, please...please."

"What score?"

"All the shit they add up at the end of the day, Bob—and as it turns out, I probably still owe you some." He extended the necklace again, "Just don't do anything stupid out there."

And so Robert took the necklace with a shrug and slid it over his head, smirking the boyish smirk that both of them once knew so well.

And that, because it was all that could be said on that cold morning in Elting, New York, was that.

———————

The Thruway had been plowed, but there was still a gloppy mess on the road, speeding tractor trailers and, as he muttered to himself as if he was speaking to Garrison, those horses' asses in Escalades and Ford Expeditions splattering salt and melting ice on the windshield, all that shit clinging to the wipers until they were useless and he had to pull over and scrape them clean with his near-frostbitten fingers.

There were four-five-six then seven loops of the Allman Brothers' "Ramblin' Man" providing the soundtrack from the Elting exit to the Harriman tolls where he got caught up in the loop of the cross-country fantasy that never happened, the one that always began with him herding the family into a Winnebago with strollers, bikes, boogie boards, kayaks precariously bungeed to the roof. "Pony Boy" now playing through to "Can't Lose"… to "Come and Go"…to "Bougainvillea"…the five Tevises riding over a hill on a clear blue morning, laughing together, his elbow out the window.…

And now here he was, in the Winnebago, switching the iPod to The Boss, putting on the right blinker and taking Exit 15 to Route 287, the snow now gone from the roadway. He cranked the beast up to 70 miles per hour as he passed the Wayne turnoff where his parents lived for the last decades of their lives, past the Bernardsville exit and the Bernardsville Quality Inn where he and Brenda Holloway spent the best stolen weekend of their ill-fated affair, turned onto Rte 78 West through Bridgewater, out of Jersey and into Pennsylvania, Easton, Bethlehem, Allentown, slowing at the Shartlesville exit, briefly considered stopping to take a cell phone picture of the big green exit sign and sending it to Alyssa and Sam—who, before all that happened happened, would have laughed out loud at the name.

"Shartlesville," he said out loud and snickered, a little less morose than he was moments before. How many times, he wondered, had the five of them sat around the dining room table as Alyssa and Sam played out that scene verbatim from "Along Came Polly":

Hoffman character (Alyssa): We gotta go, dude!

Ben Stiller character (Sam): Why?

Alyssa: It's an emergency!

Sam: What?

Alyssa (whispers): I sharted, dude.

Sam: What's that?

Alyssa: Sharted!

Sam: Huh?

Alyssa: I farted and a little shit came out!

Sam: You are the most disgusting person I've ever met in my life.

Every time they laughed, and everyone laughed, as if it was the first time any of them had heard it.

Robert cupped the phone in his hand, felt its weight, but then put it back down on the console. This was not the time to reinvent the moment. He would never again speak with Marion; and neither Alyssa nor Sam would appreciate the message from him—any message from him; and Beryl, well, Beryl was another story altogether.

Time to blast *Thunder Road* and *Born to Run* over and over and over and over and over again.

––––––––––

With the sun already disappearing behind the Bear Pond Mountains outside of Hagerstown, Maryland, Robert began looking for some out of the way place to stop for the night.

He'd already learned—in two trial jaunts to the Finger Lakes and North Hero Island in Lake Champlain over the previous autumn—that campgrounds were no place for depressed, quiet, or ponderous older men. As he told Garrison, you have to smile and crack jokes with your temporary neighbors or they'll just keep inviting you over for a beer and buckets of bright orange Cheetos until they beat you down—and sucked the cells out of your brain.

It didn't matter now, though. There were no campgrounds open in February, so Robert drove another two hours and, after spotting the massive sign from 81, pulled into a Wal-Mart parking lot outside of Staunton, Virginia. The store was closed, but the tall parking lights were bright and, although wary, he was relieved to see that he was not alone.

In a mostly deserted lot, he rolled past a small outpost of "Good Sam" RVs huddled together like an old wagon train, and then swung around to the other side of the building, in between the big spotlights where he figured he could see the others but remain hidden himself. He cut the headlights, killed the motor, walked the five or six steps it took to get back to the control panel, flipped on the generator, and lowered himself to the bench that, later on, would convert into his bed for the night.

With his elbows on the little table and his rough chin resting on his hands, clasped together in a semblance of prayer, Robert found himself in a place he'd never been before, a kind of "timeless void" (his journal words) in which there was no past, no future, just the utterly ordinary present that, he imagined, "an ordinary man might find sitting at an ordinary table on some nondescript night. A figure," he wrote in his messy script, "not unlike the solitary man passing time at the counter in Edward Hopper's 'Nighthawks.'"

This is what my life has come to, he thought and reached up to slide the journal onto the shelf.

And so he felt, in that singularly unexpected and unspectacular moment, that he might never get up from that bench. It seemed that there was nothing that could move him; not a woman, a book, a song, a call from his children, a stabbing pain in his back, a rumbling in his intestines, nothing. He would just sit here, neither here nor there, waiting for morning, waiting for death. So he just stared into the dark window, the reflection revealing nothing beyond itself.

Robert hadn't counted on hunger, though. Simple hunger, that is. Growling stomach hunger. Which was when he reached up and slid the journal off the shelf, the pen falling on the linoleum floor. "… not that bullshit psychic hunger I spent my life hashing and rehashing with clients," he wrote. "Not that awful gnawing hunger that drives people into affairs, into addictions, into institutions, the kind of hunger that even led a few of them to place a noose around their necks or toss a handful of Seconols down their throats or place the barrel of a gun in their mouths." He could have named them all, but stopped writing.

No, there was nothing psychological about his stomach growling. This, he assured himself, was just hunger, plain and simple. He was belly hungry. He hadn't eaten since the morning. Or was it the night before? He didn't remember.

Chapter Three

Still sitting there in the Winnebago, it took Robert another minute or more to convince himself that he needed to move. Pressing his bulk down on his palms and rising, dizzy at first, his chest rising and falling, he stood in front of the marvelously well-designed pantry of the Winnebago, where nothing would move or shake or break when the vehicle rounded corners or stopped short. There Robert found everything he would need for dinner. He pulled a can of Dinty Moore beef stew off the top shelf, an odd choice, he snickered (I'm snickering! he thought), for a man who was a practicing and self-righteous vegetarian until late last spring.

He held the can in his hand, impressed with the heft of it, the way it fit his stiff and swollen palm, the straightforward unpretentious label, no claims for health or equanimity or regular bowel movements or cancer protections, just a meal that would alleviate for a brief time his animal hunger with potatoes, carrots, and animal by-products.

Robert liked knowing where everything was in the Winnebago, the can opener in the second drawer, the pot in the base cabinet, three plates in the cabinet above the burners, a loaf of white bread in the drawer below the forks, spoons and knives, two pounds of butter in the tiny fridge, the stew spooned out into the pot, the pot slid onto the burner, the blue, red and white can tossed into the sink to be rinsed later on.

And with nothing else in the world to do, Robert stood at the stove trying to be patient until the stew finally began simmering, then spooned it out on the plate in between two slices of buttered bread. Next he ripped a single paper towel from the roll beneath the cabinet and, plate in hand and looking all around the small traveling apartment, sat back down on the bench.

The first mouthful of stew was so tasty, so satisfying, that his lip began to tremble with a joyful sadness he had never before known. To calm himself, he spooned another, and then another, then a bite of buttered white Freihoffer's bread, a sip of water, and then, out of nowhere it seemed, there was someone tapping on the door. The knock knock was timid at first, then becoming louder and more insistent.

Robert considered not answering, but as the lights were on and the generator was buzzing, there really was no faking not being home—and as his experiences at the campgrounds taught him, whoever it was wouldn't stop until he opened the door. He got up from the bench, wiped his mouth on the napkin, brushed his hands on the back of his pants, and just as the second series of rising knocks came, opened the door.

Outside were two smiling hippie kids, maybe eighteen maybe twenty maybe older, bundled into what looked like bulbous 1980s down jackets, a blond girl with a full face and dreds, and a dark-haired, bearded boy with a red doo-rag. "Hi!" she said with maybe a little too much perk.

The boy smiled with embarrassment, "I'm really, we're really sorry to bother you, but…we're over there with our friends in that bus." He pointed behind to a yellow and red school bus. "And we're making pancakes and ran out of eggs—and the Wally is closed," pointing the other way toward the darkened Wal-Mart store. The boy nodded agreeably with himself. So did Robert, nodding and smiling, though he held the doorknob tight in his hand, heart pounding, glancing over their shoulders to see if anyone was coming.

Then, like a tag team match, the girl took over: "So we were wondering if you would lend us, like, two or three eggs—we'll pay you back tomorrow when the store opens—or maybe you'd be welcome to join us and we'll make you bacon and pancakes and all the good coffee you can drink. My name is Clover and his name is Mountain Eagle."

Then the boy was back smiling and shaking his shaggy head, "We're really really sorry to bother you, sir— we're just stoppin' here on our way down to Asheville. I really hope you don't think we mean you any harm—"

"The thought crossed my mind," Robert admitted. But he didn't say that he was headed to Asheville, too.

"Oh no, no no, we're lovers, not fighters, Mr. __?" The boy smiled again—or was it a smirk, Robert wondered, understanding in that made-for-TV Ray Liotta or Kevin Bacon moment that there was no way to escape this suddenly perilous situation, alone in this dark and cold parking lot, so far away from all the other Wal-Mart freeloaders. If this Clover and Mountain Whatever, Bonnie and Clyde, had malicious intentions—and worse, friends back in the red and yellow bus—he would have no way to save himself, no matter what he did, no matter how hard he fought, how loud he screamed.

And now the really surprising thing was that idea didn't frighten him as much as he thought it would. Or should.

And a few moments later it didn't scare him at all. "Bob. My name is Bob." Dr. Robert Tevis had never called himself Bob, even as a kid. He was Robert. Garrison was the only one who called him Bob. Or Bobby. He remained standing in the open doorway.

"Y'know, Bob, you look a little like my dad," the boy said. "His name is George. So where you headed?"

He parted his lips, still smiling, but didn't say anything.

"Aw, Bobby, I'm sorry…none of my business. We're all just on the road. That's cool. I sometimes forget myself."

"No, no, no…son," he said, unable to say Mountain Eagle, "I just drew a blank for a moment. I'm going to Asheville, too. I have a daughter down there. Teaches at Warren Wilson. Y'know—"

Clover slapped her knee and laughed. "That is the coolest college in the whole freakin' world. She must be something."

And without a clue as to why, that nebulous connection emboldened Robert Tevis to invite the two hippies in to his Winnebago. Something he certainly never would have done before he left Elting. Something he wouldn't have done fifteen minutes ago. More than anything, it seemed, his old life suddenly behind him, he was actually curious to see where this chance meeting would go, good or bad. "Very cool!" cooed the girl as soon as she stepped up into the vehicle. "Very, very cool," stammered the boy who closed the door behind him and glanced toward the queen-size bed.

Clover noticed the beef stew first, "Oh, you're eating…I'm so sorry we bothered you!"

"No no no, that's fine, Clover. Really. Let me check to see if I have any eggs." Robert knew full well that he had a dozen in the refrigerator, each in its own little container with a lid. He turned his back on the pair and, half expecting to be knocked unconscious or feel a gun at his nape from behind, opened the little fridge. Without turning, he called back, "Three eggs did you say?"

"Well," the boy began, "three would be great, Bobby, but four would do even better!" He thought Clover looked embarrassed.

And so Robert gathered up six eggs and found a plastic bag to put them in. "This should tide you over."

The two kids were effusive in their thanks, inviting him again to join them and their friends for a feast and, huddled shoulder to shoulder together outside the open door, promising over and over again to repay him for the eggs, "as soon as the Wally opens up again."

Robert assured them it was fine, that it was his donation to their trip, but they promised again to repay him—and, looking back and forth to each other, invited him over to the bus, even if he didn't want to eat. "Well, we'll be just sittin' around listening to tunes, drinkin' some beer, " Mountain Eagle laughed. "I bet you like to soak up the suds, right Bob?"

Robert shrugged, affably enough he thought. And figured that would be the last of Mountain Eagle and Clover.

Chapter Four

Marion Barton Tevis and Jed Blackstone had spent the last five days in San Jose buying a 1986 Toyota Corolla, taking care of visas and other such legal matters, eating plate after plate of gallo pinto and cassado, drinking bottle after bottle of Imperial cervesa, wandering hand in hand through the narrow streets of what seemed like an endless barrio, and each night, except the last, making slow quiet deliberate love in their musty air-conditioned room at the Hotel Aranjuez near the airport.

Once they left the obscure boundaries of the capital city, the drive along 27 past Ananos, San Rafael, Guacima Ariba, and on and on was full of ruts and roadblocks, U-turns and mud, and some of the most glorious vistas that Jed, who had never been west of the Mississippi, had ever seen. And Marion, who was returning to Costa Rica for the first time since the "revelation" about her husband's affair, hadn't been this excited, this scared, this giddy, since her freshman year at Wisconsin, sitting on the terrace behind the Rathskellar, looking out on the windy Lake Mendota, the ripples moving in across the vast vast expanse, small whitecaps lapping at the shore, willing her wonderful and awful life to begin.

There was nothing like Costa Rica in her past life, not in those small Nebraska ponds that anyone who was anyone could easily swim across, not in Elting where the mountain lakes were frigid all summer long, not on Long Beach Island where all those sweating, oily bodies made the water uninviting. She squealed like the girl she once was when they cruised over the top of a jaw-dropping mountain pass, the blue blue blue "Oh my God, Jeddy!"

blue Pacific appeared in the distance. "Oh, Jed!" she cried again and slapped his bare thigh, stomping her feet on the floorboards of the rusty old Toyota.

Jed Blackstone, the former pastor of the Elting Reformed Church, was no less moved by the sight of the ocean than was Marion. But it was not in his nature to be so expressive; and, besides, the weight of what they were doing, the vast burdens left behind after what they had done, and the more immediate fear that the car would crumble under Marion's stomping feet would have kept him closemouthed, nodding and smiling in appreciation as one does in the presence of an exuberant child.

"Oh, Jeddy, isn't this just the most beautiful thing you've ever seen?" she cooed.

He reached over for her smooth knee, slid his palm up to the hem of her shorts. "It is…it sure is, Mari."

She didn't miss his hesitation—she'd already grown used to it (a welcome relief at first from Robert's endless explanations and analyses and what he called "life lessons")—and grabbed the road map from the door pocket and traced the road from Tarcoles to Jaco to Quepos to Manuel Antonio.

It was late in the afternoon when they arrived tired and sweaty at the Si Como No Resort, right outside Parque Nacional Manuel Antonio. Marion got out her small leather address book and tried calling Carlos Estrada, but he didn't answer the phone at the Quepos Real Estate office. So while Jed stayed back at the car, Marion went into the motel office and paid for a room.

After they unloaded the car—Marion gathering in her arms the camera, the laptop, the backpack with all their documents, and the woven basket she bought in San Jose that now contained snacks and bottles of water; Jed grabbing the big hiking pack and Marion's oversized suitcase—they walked up one flight of outside steps to their room, pushed closed the sodden door and together plopped down on the queen-size bed, soaked with sweat and a little bit giddy, the rising panic, like an incoming squall, just behind their throats.

When they both grew quiet, the voices of monkeys and birds punctuating the silence, Jed rolled over and placed his hand on her round shoulder and then, moments later, turning his hand and sliding the back of his fingers up over her flushed cheeks, her forehead, tracing her strong jawline to her chin, now moving down her long neck, her full breasts under the thin tanktop, her soft belly, his fingers turning over as easily as aster leaves, now cupping her breast and burying his lips in her warm neck. "Let's make love," he whispered.

A smile that was not a smile flickered across her face. "Not now," she said, kissing his forehead, "I want to walk around the jungle, my love...see the monkeys and the lizards...I want a drink, two drinks, gooey sweet drinks full of syrup and rum, with pink umbrellas...and I want to walk the beach, up and down, until I feel like I'm really here." She lifted his hand off her breast and clasped it to her cheek. "Is that okay, Jedi?"

"We can do all that," he said, moving his leg over hers, "but first this," pressing himself to her.

"Later," she whispered, her voice a little less lilting. "Promise. But first I need that drink and a deep breath—and a lotta, lotta sand between my toes...and definitely a shower."

Jed rolled onto his back and sighed, staring up at the wooden ceiling and trying, in his own remarkably unpracticed way, to make her feel guilty for denying him. But Marion, who knew her way well around this intimate territory, was quickly up and off the soft bed, moving around the tiled floor, collecting the camera, the binoculars, her hat, a bottle of water, and the small backpack. "Let's go down to the beach, Jedi," she said, wriggling his toes as she passed by the foot of the bed.

———————

Early the next morning—after a sweaty night that was never going to include making love, Marion being unapologetically weary and gassy from the two umbrella drinks, not to mention even more gallo pinto and cassado—Jed was up, dressed, and out the door before seven, nearly tripping on a green iguana lazing on the path down to the open air lobby. He walked along the gravel and dirt road, down from the hotel toward the park and, farther along, the beach, empty except for some older couples walking hand in hand at the edge of the powder-blue surf.

He'd been here in Manuel Antonio on a Habitat for Humanity mission and knew that in a few hours the beach would be full of activity, street vendors up on the sidewalk, a couple of massage tables, surfers, volleyball players, little boys kicking soccer balls, young men with backpacks full of ceramic pots to sell, half-dressed tourists in chaise lounges, red frozen daiquiris in their hands. But for now, he could slip off the flip-flops—Marion made him leave behind what she called his Jesus sandals and bought him some Reefs—to walk the beach alone and, for the first time in what seemed a lifetime, not feel crowded in, consumed by little brothers and sisters wanting this or that and, a few memory-less years, by congregants waiting outside his door to share their woes or their failures or, worse, their smiling self-satisfied reports of their own small, petty, nearly evil triumphs over evil itself.

Standing at the edge of the surf, Jed Blackstone turned and scanned the hillside, from left to right, right to left, looking, looking, looking, and when he found the cross he knew must be there, walked back to the street, stepped back into the flip-flops and followed a sand road up to the small white building, a simple white cross over the door.

The path through the overgrown grass up to the front porch was lined with stones painted white. The door was locked. He knocked three times and waited, his hands clasped behind his back. No one came.

Jed walked around the back of the small wooden building, a capuchin monkey swinging through the trees seemingly unperturbed by the human intruder. The rickety back door, which he could easily have muscled open, was locked as well, so he sat down on the rotting wooden landing, clasped his hands together, closed his eyes, and lowered his head on top of his thumbs.

It took a while for the words to come. "Please forgive me, Father," he said finally, "for I am a loathsome sinner. I am a home wrecker. I am a hypocrite. I am a fornicator. I am the betrayer of my flock. I am Judas. I am simmering with lust. I am lost in this ungodly love for a woman whose love and faith I have not earned. Please forgive me, Father."

When he opened his eyes, a short old man stood nearby, wearing leather sandals (the kind Marion had thrown out), khaki shorts, a white embroidered shirt, and a cheap white Panama hat. His face was round, pockmarked, and, although kindly, seemed to bear a constant scowl. He spoke in impeccable English: "Son? May I help you? I am Pastor Henriquez. This is my church."

Jed stood and, in standing, towered over the old man. He held out his hand. "Jed Blackstone."

Pastor Henriquez offered a soft and fleshy squeeze. "I am pleased to make your acquaintance, Senor Blackstone. You are troubled, no?"

Jed smiled the smile of the dispossessed, an expression he had seen and ministered to time and time again. "Yes, I guess I am." He looked around the small black man at the vast tangle of bushes and big-leafed trees. "I was wondering if you would offer me a blessing?"

"Of course I will, my son, but first tell me what brings you here first thing in the morning?" The pastor looked at his watch and winked. "Most sinners are still sleeping at this hour."

There didn't seem any reason to avoid or to evade the question, especially as it was one that he had asked troubled followers hundreds, maybe thousands, of times before, sitting so smugly behind his desk in the rectory. "I was the pastor of the Elting Reformed Church in upstate New York until very recently...in the United States." He stopped then, not knowing where to go next.

The old man nodded and said, not unkindly, "I know where New York is, Pastor."

Jed pressed his lips together. "I'm sorry."

"Not as sorry as you are for something else, I assume," said Pastor Henriquez, deep lines at his eyes and cheeks as he smiled and sat down next to Jed. "So what? You fell in love with a parishioner and have moved here to escape the nasty messages on your answering machine, the un-Christian notes in your mailbox, the leers of the righteous church board members who censored you in such a public fashion?"

Jed was incredulous. "Yes! Yes! Yes! How did you...?"

"It's an old, old story, Senor Blackstone. I can tell you this already: You're not nearly the unique soul you believe yourself to be." The pastor stood up to his full height, a half-foot shorter than Jed, then winked again. "And yes, it is pitiable, a most pitiable and common story."

Jed nodded like a schoolboy, his eyes pooling.

Pastor Henriquez paused then, letting his words sink in for a few moments. "You have done grievous wrong, son, and you have much to atone for, perhaps more than you know."

The younger pastor nodded.

"You should know this, though: We may not always see eye to eye," the pastor went on, "but you are welcome here in my church and in my home. I will not turn you away."

Jed wiped his eyes as he stood and held out his hand again. "Thank you, Pastor Henriquez. Thank you with all my heart. Thank you for your blessing. I…I will not disappoint you."

The pastor grabbed hold of his smooth palms, looked up into the sea-blue watery eyes of the tall, skinny white man and said, "Yes, I suppose that is my blessing, but I am not the one you should be concerned about disappointing."

Jed glanced down again.

"Now, don't cry, Mr. Jed Blackstone, it's not manly, especially for a man of the cloth." He winked one more time. "And I hope to see you and your friend on Sunday."

Jed glanced up, "Did I mention—?"

"No."

———————————

When Jed labored back up the hill he found Marion sitting in a white plastic chair outside their motel room, sipping the strong Costa Rican coffee. She looked happy. "Where have you been?" she asked.

"Walking. Walking the beach. Just wandering around." He leaned down and kissed her on the cheek before dragging over the other plastic chair.

"Did you see anyone?"

"Here?" he said, not knowing why he was stalling. "Who would I know around here?"

Marion shrugged, "Just wondering. You were gone awhile and I figured you might have met someone."

"Nope. Just walking on the beach. It's beautiful." He glanced over and smiled at the woman for whom he had given up everything.

"Coffee?" she said, already getting up to open the warped door to their room.

Jed opened his mouth to say yes, but she had already slipped out of sight. A few moments later she returned with a Styrofoam cup, a thin plastic brown straw poking up between thumb and forefinger.

"So...?"

"So I met a minister down the road..."

"I thought you said you didn't meet anyone?"

He winced against the interrogating voice. "I guess I didn't want to talk about it."

Marion put her cup down on the stone patio. "So, go ahead, talk about it now, Jedidiah. Tell me."

He stared straight ahead then, into the tangled jungle. "It was nothing, really, just a funny-looking gnome of a country pastor, but he seemed to see right through me."

"Well, I have to say that you're pretty easy to read these days, Jedi." She reached over and squeezed his hand. "You know, you need to find the forgiveness you granted to me when I...hmmm... strayed." A churlish smile played at the edges of her mouth.

"Your husband cheated on you, Marion. You were hurt, your faith was shaken, you struck back at him with whatshisname?"

She closed her eyes. "Garrison. Jesus F. Christ, I still can't believe that I did that to Robert. That was just plain awful, Jedi. Awful of me. Awful of him. I'm still so ashamed of myself."

Jed winced again, this time at Marion taking the Lord's name in vain. After a while he gathered up his courage. "I never knew ...did your husband...did Robert ever find out?"

"No. I hope he never finds out." She looked off down toward the slice of light blue sea over the trees. "I'm sorry to admit that I planned to tell him, to find the right time to hurt him as he had hurt me, but then other things happened." There was that churlish smile again.

Jed grinned in spite of himself. Then after another sip of the coffee: "You know, I never intended—"

"I know, Jedi, we've been all through this. I didn't intend for any of it to happen, either. And I never thought you took advantage of me. In fact, I sometimes think I took advantage of you. In fact—" She withdrew her hand from his and laid it, palm up, in her lap.

He was insulted but didn't know why. "So…I guess Robert still doesn't know about Garrison?"

She finished off the cup of coffee. "No. He was hurt enough later when I told him about us—devastated, I would say—and it was pretty clear that Garrison, that gutless coward, was never going to admit betraying his oldest friend in the world, not to mention cheating on his poor invalid wife. And it just seemed cruel to pile it on."

Jed tossed the warm contents of the cup into the bushes. "Nasty tasting stuff," he said. "Anyway, the point is that I have no excuse. You were hurt to the quick, and, although it was wrong in the eyes of the Lord, you at least had some reason to strike back, to do what you did. "

She shrugged. "Maybe. And you didn't? In some ways you're the most hurt person I know."

"You've said that before, Mari, but I'm still wondering." He reached across the table, taking her hand in his, leaning over and kissing the soft skin over her knuckles. "No one betrayed me. No one had made false promises to me. But from the moment you walked into my office in the rectory, I knew I couldn't help myself. I just never knew such yearning before. And I knew I should send you away to speak with someone else, but I couldn't."

"Well, let's say I'm eternally glad you didn't. Anyway, I'm not sure you could have made me go." She got up, walked around the small table, and sidled onto his lap.

"Me too," he said. "And maybe that's the whole problem. I

just don't feel guilty enough. I want His forgiveness, but I'm not willing to change anything that happened. That's the rub, right?"

"I think the rub is that maybe we should go inside now and rub each other and try to recall what we need forgiveness for."

She got up then and taking him by the hand, led Jedidiah into their rented room.

Chapter Five

At 11 p.m., with a boyish motorboat sound riffling through his lips, Robert officially abandoned Proust for the fifth or sixth time in his life, this time closing the fat book without turning over the corner of the last page he had tried to read, dropping it on the linoleum RV floor. This time he only made it to page 32 of *Swann's Way*, having read and re-read the following sentence six or seven times:

For many years, albeit—and especially before his marriage—M. Swann the younger came often to see them at Combray, my great-aunt and grandparents never suspected that he had entirely ceased to live in the kind of society which his family had frequented, or that, under the sort of incognito which the name of Swann gave him among us, they were harbouring—with the complete innocence of a family of honest innkeepers who have in their midst some distinguished highwayman and never know it—one of the smartest members of the Jockey Club, a particular friend of the Comte de Paris and of the Prince of Wales, and one of the men most sought after in the aristocratic world of the Faubourg Saint-Germain.

He propped up his pillow and leaned back, already knowing that he was going to get dressed, walk across the cold parking lot, and knock on the door of the yellow and red school bus. He didn't know why he knew he was going to do that or why he would even want to spend some time with goofy-looking hippies in a school bus. Or why he knew he would never again pick up Proust.

Or why, at the age of sixty, he found it necessary to make

up an excuse in order to knock on the door of some vagabond hippies, holding up a plastic cup when Mountain Eagle yanked the folding door open with a concerned look on his face. "Oh man…it's you…Bob?"

"Bob," he said, raising the cup a few inches higher in the air.

"We thought it was, you know—" he started to say something, but apparently thought better of it.

"Well, this time it's my turn to apologize," Robert said. "I was wondering if you had a few tablespoons of sugar for my tea—I saw the light on in your bus or I wouldn't have—"

"No apologies, Bob," he heard Clover say from inside somewhere. "Come in out of the cold."

Mountain Eagle leaned out and held out a hand, coupling soft flesh to soft flesh and pulling the older man up into the school bus, which Robert immediately recognized (mostly from an unhappy visit to see Beryl some years before in Yellow Springs) as reeking of patchouli and looking just like he'd imagined Ken Kesey's mess of a bus back in the day: tie-dye sheets over the windows, sticky pots on the makeshift stove, overflowing ashtrays, Indian bedspreads bunched up on the two folded futons—now serving as pillows for what might have been called the conversation pit if this was a 1950s suburban living room—bottles of cheap beer all around, a plate of brownies as the centerpiece.

Clover introduced Robert to Phoenix and Savannah, telling them that he was "the dude that lent us the eggs." Neither got up, but both smiled and in unison, it seemed, offered Bob a "V" with upturned fingers. Both were filthy. Phoenix's arm was covered in angry tattoos. Savannah, multiple-pierced, just looked sleepy. Robert responded with a sheepish grin, open palm, and more of the original lie: "Yeah, I was just making some tea for myself and found that I forgot the sugar…" He held up the cup again.

"Well," Savannah laughed out of her stupor, revealing a missing tooth in an otherwise Sicilian dark and beautiful sculpted face, "eggs for sugar…that's a good trade. Would you like a brownie to go along with that tea?" She laughed again. "That's what we used your eggs for."

"Yeah," Clover quickly interjected from the pit, "we decided against the pancakes. Come in, take a load off, Bob."

"I…I don't want to intrude, I just—and besides, you don't want to be sitting around with an old man."

"Don't be ridiculous," she countered. "I'm sick of these characters—we've been ridin' together since Burlington and I'd love to talk about something other than how great Jerry and Phil were. Sit down."

Robert knew just enough to understand she was talking about the Grateful Dead, but that was about it. She scrunched over, threw a worn pillow on the floor and patted the futon, "Sit here."

As soon as Robert had lowered his bulk down to the too-low futon and listed backward, Savannah picked up the plate and leaned across with her offering. "They're really good," she said and glanced at Phoenix with a thin, close-lipped smile.

Patting his stomach, Robert said something stupid (he thought) about his boyish figure, but Savannah insisted: "C'mon, Bob, one won't kill you and they're really tasty—Mountain Eagle's like a professional chef—and besides, it'll give us a chance to get to know each other. That's what bein' on the road is all about."

He felt trapped now, just like he'd been with the insistent RV folks at the Finger Lakes and North Hero Island campgrounds. Reaching over the divide, he picked up the smallest brownie on the plastic plate. He glanced sideways at Clover, who smiled sweetly and nodded, and then at Mountain Eagle, who had by then plopped down on his right.

Mountain Eagle looked uncomfortable. He turned to his fellow travelers and said, "This isn't cool." They seemed instantly deflated by this unexpected call to conscience. Then he told Robert, "Before you eat that brownie, Bob, you should know it's not a regular brownie."

Robert pressed his lips together and tilted his head, adopting his stock psychoanalytic pose, the one that would hide his emergent disdain while encouraging clients to talk a little more about whatever was troubling them.

"It's what we call a magic brownie, Bobby, if you get my drift," Mountain Eagle said with a grin.

"I guess I've been drifting in that direction," Robert said as nonchalantly as possible. That was no lie.

"Ever smoke weed, Bob?" Phoenix said with a sneer. "You know, Mary Jane? Dank? Doobage? Ganja? Wacky Backy?"

With the same kind of resolve he once faked for Marion when they climbed the steep and rocky Dunn Falls in Jamaica, his heart thudding so hard he thought it might explode, Robert took a big bite out of the brownie and smiled broadly. "I was around in the Sixties, y'know. This is not new to me."

Of course, it was all that—and more. Robert had smoked something that someone called marijuana once with Garrison and his fraternity brothers in Madison, and although they didn't really get high, they giggled a lot and pretended to have the munchies. Also, he and Garrison had been over the mountain to Woodstock in '69, but there'd been no hippie buses involved, no hash brownies, no acid, no wild naked dancing, and, when the muddy concert was over, it was just the two boys again in Robert's father's Chrysler New Yorker, heading back to hot showers in their tidy village houses and summer jobs as Outdoor Recreation Workers at the famed Mohonk Mountain House, which didn't even allow liquor on the premises.

Mountain Eagle leaned over then and patted Robert on the back: "As Jerry said, 'As far as I'm concerned, it's like I say, drugs are not the problem. Other stuff is the problem.'"

Robert nodded, he thought knowingly, and took another bite of the brownie, his natural reticence slowly drifting out of the portal that suddenly opened on the top of his skull. "My daughter Beryl likes the Dead," he said, not knowing whether that was true at all, but mostly to show them he knew that Jerry was Jerry Garcia.

Phoenix sat up and leaned across, an angry sneer lifting his upper lip. "But you don't?"

Robert first looked over at Clover and then shrugged like a shy boy. "I actually don't know what I like." It was the first unabashedly honest or true thing he said to the grungy group.

"Maybe that's why you're on the road, Bobby," Clover said and patted his thick thigh, "to meet folks like us. We know what we like. That's why we're on the road. It's a righteous journey." She glanced over at her friends. "And I think you're a righteous guy."

Mountain Eagle nodded his head slowly, once twice three times, "Amen." He reached underneath the futon and slid out a ragged-looking paperback book, Jerry Garcia's round face on the cover. "Here," he said, thumbing through the yellowed pages: "'If we had any nerve at all, if we had any real balls as a society, or whatever you need, whatever quality you need, real character, we would make an effort to really address the wrongs in this society, righteously.' It's about being righteous, Bobby. Here," he said, extending the plate, "have another one."

Robert obliged. And from then on, it became easier and easier, more and more like lava flowing out of the volcano, as he got higher and higher with each bite of the second brownie, to feel at home in this alien spaceship—as he soon came to envision it—to talk with these kids, somehow *his* kids, he began to imagine, sharing various truths of his past, including the affair with Brenda Holloway ("Bobby Bob!" cried Savannah, "you are a hound dog!"), as they shared with him some truly shocking life stories, none of which he remembered the following morning when he woke up in his own bed in his own recreational vehicle, the world spinning, or not really spinning, he realized, just rumbling as if it were moving at a great speed down the highway.

Which it was.

Robert sat up, fully dressed, fully confused, at the precipitous edge of panic. "Hey!" he yelled swinging his numb legs around. Two seconds later, Clover was standing, all bright and cheery, at his side.

"Hey back at ya, sleepyhead!" she said, her full-face smile and strawberry blond dreads like the rising sun. "I thought you said you were just going to close your eyes for fifteen minutes."

He rubbed his eyes. "What's going on? Where are we?"

"Where are we, Mountain?" she called over her shoulder to the front of the speeding vehicle.

The blurry scene gained some definition. "And why the hell is he driving my van?"

Mountain Eagle called back from the driver's seat, mixed with "All Along the Watchtower" reverberating through the speakers, "We're just comin' up to Roanoke, Bobby—not too fuckin' shabby, I'd say!"

Robert turned to Clover, dizzy now, looking up into what could only be called a beatific smile. "Are you kidnapping me?"

Clover laughed that deep-throated laugh he had already come to recognize as hers and sat down on the mattress. "No no no, Bob...don't you remember that you asked us to join you on the way down to Asheville?"

He shook his head. "No."

"You did."

"So, you're not going to—"

She put her bare arm around his warm, rounded shoulder. "We're not going to do anything except meet Phoenix and Savannah in Asheville." Then she called out to Mountain, "Hey, I told you not to let him have that third brownie!"

Chapter Six

Robert turned up the volume on the iPod—Nina Simone crooning "Please Don't Let Me Be Misunderstood"—trying to drown out what he now assumed were the sounds of lovemaking in the back of the Winnebago. He was five miles from the Warren Wilson College exit off I-40.

When he was two miles away, he called over his shoulder, "Clover, Mountain, we're almost there!" And the two of them were up front in a flash, fully dressed and overflowing with enthusiasm, Mountain Eagle leaping into the passenger seat and Clover flying onto his lap. She was already phoning their friends when he turned off Exit 55, Asheville/Swannanoa. "We're here!" she cried. "Okay...okay...okay...remember this," turning to Mountain Eagle, "it's the Wal-Mart right off Tunnel Road. Or left off Tunnel Road."

"We're making a left onto Tunnel," Robert said.

"Bob said we're making a left onto Tunnel," she chirped into the cell. "We'll see you in...what?...ten freakin' minutes!" She flipped the cell closed and looked over at the driver. "Y'know, this is gonna sound a little crazy, Bob, but I know I'm gonna be missin' you."

"Yeah?" he said, unable to suppress the boyish grin he knew was spreading across his face.

"Yeah."

Robert glanced to the side and saw that her eyes were now watery. He reached over and squeezed her hand, wondering what in the hell he'd said or done to these two strange kids—so different than his own children—and why they seemed to like him. Why, in fact, they hadn't dumped his sorry ass on the roadside and taken his RV.

————————————

Ten minutes on, in the far back of the Wal-Mart parking lot, Robert parked the RV and lowered himself out of the driver's seat. He stretched his aching back and sore hips and walked over to the bus where Mountain Eagle and Clover were already laughing with Phoenix and Savannah—no doubt, he was sure, about his lost night and his fretful awakening.

"Bobby Bob!" Phoenix shouted, a signal for the others to shut up. "How goes it, my man?"

"Better," he said, not sure what comparison he was making. He held out his swollen hand, and Phoenix grabbed it with a quick, languid shake.

Robert slid his fingers into his back pocket, mostly to rub off the clamminess that lingered there from Phoenix. He looked at the four hippie children, all suddenly tongue-tied, now waiting for him to leave them alone. "So...Phoenix, Savannah, Mountain, Clover," nodding and smiling at each one as he said their name, "I just want to say thanks for your hospitality last night, apologies if I said or did something that insulted anyone." He looked at each one again, and when no one said anything, the four kids just smiling at him like he belonged in a mental institution, Robert raised his free hand in an air toast, "Here's to brand new beginnings, new friends, and, um...," glancing around at the crowded mall parking lot, "some...'warm summer breezes, French wine and cheeses' on your way to that festival in Austin."

"Buffett, yeah!" Mountain Eagle laughed, but the others didn't get the connection. No matter, Robert thought, raising his swollen hand even higher in the air. He was done explaining himself. It was indeed time to move on. He then shook Savannah's small, soft hand. She went up on tiptoes and gave him a peck on the cheek.

Phoenix, now standing on the first step of the bus, called out with a smirk, "Rock on, Bro!"

Robert folded his thick fingers into a fist and thrust it into the air, to Savannah's delight. And when he turned around, Mountain Eagle was right behind. "I know we only met a day ago, man, but I'd ride with you any day"—and with that he wrapped his long, thin arms around Robert's shoulders and hugged him, a wholly generous hug that, later that day, made Robert wonder how long, how many years it had been since Sam hugged him that way. Or that he had hugged his only son that way.

Then it was Clover's turn; she was bawling by the time he turned to her. "I'm sorry for crying like this, Bobby, I just feel bad that we're saying good-bye already." He put his arms around her thin shoulders and felt her hot breath on his neck while she sobbed. He waited until the sobbing stopped and then gently took her face in his palms, kissing her on the forehead.

"We'll see you again somewhere," she said. "I know we will."

"Definitely," he lied despite his recent intention to tell the truth, the whole truth, for the rest of his life. "I definitely will, sweet girl. I know I will." He let her go, as relieved as he was sad to wave good-bye, to watch Mountain Eagle and then Clover disappearing behind the folding doors

---

With the lingering memory of Clover sobbing in his arms, Robert drove up Tunnel Road in the midst of the kind of belly-deep sadness he hadn't known since his mother died when he was nine. His own kids had not held on to him like that since they were barely in their teens, if then. Christ, Alyssa barely offered a cool cheek to kiss when they met. And while Sam still hugged him when they met up, it was all pretty lifeless, no emotion behind it. Which brought him finally away from Clover to Beryl, as he made a left on Warren Wilson Road.

Robert hadn't spoken with his daughter, his baby girl, in more than a year. Before it all started falling apart, Beryl was his little pal, the freckled tomboy who'd drive with him to the dump on Saturdays, who'd accompany him to Mets games long after most teenage girls wouldn't be found dead in public with their dads. Who, after she went off to Antioch to study biology, became his nemesis, the one he couldn't get to listen to good sense.

Now that he counted backward, it was closer to a year and a half that he last saw her, on a windy August day down on Hatteras, when he advised her, once again, against "forsaking your career" (and a new teaching position in Field Biology at UNC-Asheville) in order to move to Milwaukee with her boyfriend, Stephen Sutherland.

Beryl and Stephen had met at a rent party in Boston two years before and fallen quickly in love. He was just back from the Peace Corps and was entering Harvard Divinity School. Beryl was a TA at Boston University, a semester away from beginning her dissertation on the reintroduction of fisher cats into the Shawangunk Mountains. Two years later, Beryl had her PhD and a job offer at Warren Wilson College, starting second semester. The problem: Stephen had just been accepted into a PhD theology program at Marquette and there was nothing comparable in Asheville.

Robert couldn't understand why she was following Stephen to Milwaukee. "You need to take care of yourself, to consider your own career."

"We've already been through all this, Dad. I'm twenty-six, I have a doctorate, and I'm perfectly capable of taking care of myself without your input."

"But what the hell are you going to do in Milwaukee?" he snorted.

"Well, we've been through this, too. I've already been offered two jobs in Milwaukee," she said. "I'll be adjuncting at UW-M and Marquette—and Stephen has an assistantship—and when something more permanent opens up, I'm sure I'll be first in line to get it."

"How do you know that?"

"We'll be fine, Dad."

Robert winced as he drove up over a rise, remembering sitting up on the blanket that day and, looking across at his youngest daughter, going into his psychotherapist's bag of tricks: "I think you're sabotaging yourself, Beryl. I don't think you know what you're doing."

She pointed her finger at him. "Watch it!"

"The Asheville job is a great opportunity."

Beryl snagged her towel and slung it around her neck with a rueful smile. "And what do you know about Asheville or field biology?"

"I don't know anything about field Biology or Asheville," he said, "but I know a thing or two about human behavior."

"And?"

"And you moving to Milwaukee has all the earmarks of someone who is denying herself the chance to follow her own dream. Textbook self-effacing personality."

"Like Mom?"

He grimaced at that. "No. Not like Mom at all. She made her own decisions. You, on the other hand, seem to—"

"Seem to what?"

"Well, if you ask me, it seems that you defer to everything Stephen asks of you. And, my dear, there's a price to be paid for that. Years and years of unrequited entitlement that brings unhappy, middle-aged women to professionals like me."

She shook her head, the wind blowing her long hair. "It's just stunning how much you don't know about me."

"I know you better than you know yourself, Beryl. And you're acting like a child."

Her eyes grew wide and she looked like she was going to cry. "I'm done here," she said.

"What?"

"You heard me, I'm done."

Robert reached over to grabbed Beryl's thin arm, preventing her from rising. "What do you mean?"

"I mean I'm done sitting here with you. I'm done listening to your endlessly smug psychobabble. I have a goddamn PhD and I'm done with you treating me like I'm a four-year-old. I'm done with you treating me like a neurotic client. I'm done with you phony self-righteousness. I'm just done—and don't you dare try to stop me from leaving!"

And with that, she yanked her arm out of his grasp and walked away, a towel in one hand, the folded chair in the other, striding up and over the dune and out of sight.

He remembered then, with renewed remorse, how he didn't call after her. How he wouldn't call after his impudent child. How he thought that would be wrong. If he had learned anything from his years of psychoanalytic practice, it was that people need time to collect themselves after emotional outbursts. To see things with a clear head. To make amends. Sometimes even to apologize for their harsh—and unfair—words.

So Robert, who was by then rarely surprised by anyone's behavior, was shocked when he wandered back to their rental cottage some time later—the same one they'd been renting for years—expecting to pop the top on a couple of icy Coronas and hand one to her (thus demonstrating that he did indeed regard her as an adult, an equal) so they could talk on the upper deck about the self-defeating implications of going to Milwaukee, Wisconsin, and the alternative options for maintaining her relationship with Stephen Sunderland. In a quiet and reasoned manner. So she could see the wisdom of his argument.

Robert had waited nearly an hour before leaving the beach, fidgeting, trying to read a nearly unreadable biography of Karen Horney, occasionally racing into the surf, diving into a wave or two, then slogging back to the empty blanket. Rehearsing his opening lines for when he got back to the cottage.

But when he stepped to the top of the dune he saw instantly that Beryl's car was not in the driveway. He found Marion sitting alone in the small living room. She had been crying.

"Where's Beryl?"

Marion glared at him, her eyes bloodshot. "She packed her things and left ten minutes ago. Something about having to meet with someone in Asheville."

"Asheville? I thought—"

"I don't know, Robert. She spoke with Stephen and said she was headed off to Asheville."

"But I thought she was going to Milwaukee?"

Marion walked out on the deck and he followed. "I thought so, too, but apparently something convinced her otherwise."

"Perhaps she finally surrendered to reason," he said adopting the psychoanalytic voice. "We had an argument on the beach."

Marion gave him that old look of deep annoyance. "I know."

Robert sat down in the rocking chair. "Do you think I finally got through to her?"

She got up then, walked into the kitchen, and opened the refrigerator to begin making dinner. "No, Robert. No, I definitely don't think you got through to her."

"I wouldn't be so sure," he said.

"Either way, she said she'd call when she got there."

———————

But Beryl didn't call.

And she didn't call the next day either. Or the next. And, out of principle or hurt feelings—he couldn't tell which—all these months later, Robert still wouldn't call her.

Sam told him when Beryl emailed him and Alyssa two weeks later to let them know she was fine, that classes were starting at UNC-Asheville and that she would be in touch. But, according to Sam, she said nothing about her decision to go to Asheville, other than she was happy to be there—and Stephen would be joining her as soon as he tied up a bunch of loose ends.

Then, a week later she called Marion on her cell and apologized for storming out, and for not calling, her voice cheery, eventually offering up the catchall explanation that she had had a lot on her mind what with the change in plans, finding an apartment, her first classes just starting, Stephen moving down, and the fight with her father, "…that arrogant SOB."

There was a pause on the line then, "And what you told me about you and him, Mom. That was the killer."

Trapped, as she so often was, between her husband and her children, Marion pleaded, "He's sick with worry, Beryl. Why don't you just call him—he's at his office—and tell him you're okay."

"You tell him I'm okay," she said. "And I am okay. I'm just not ready to talk to him, not now. I just keep imagining him and that woman. I could forgive him anything but that. Anything but that."

And that was that.

For nearly a year and a half.

Eventually Robert abandoned his psychoanalytic principles—

it took until the end of September—and called her. She didn't answer.

Or call back.

And having thus stepped over his well-honed practice of paternal restraint, he phoned every day for several weeks into mid-October, but Beryl never picked up. (He supposed—wished, but not wished—that she never listened to the weepy messages he left around Halloween, their favorite holiday.) He also filled her in-box with what he called Dad-Spam and with his friend Garrison's help, a daily or twice-daily text message.

By November he was calling once a week on Sundays, in dutiful fashion, like he was the kid and she the parent, but by then he had stopped leaving messages, hanging up when he heard the voicemail message. Garrison patiently explained that Beryl would know that he had called, that she would know he had not forsaken her.

That he would never forsake her.

That he would call her every Sunday for the rest of his life.

But there was still no answer.

Robert knew that Beryl had not forsaken the rest of the family, though. He'd been told by Sam and Alyssa that she did keep up with them occasionally on email and Facebook; and about once a week, through the fall, Marion reported, over another mostly silent dinner, that she'd heard from Beryl that morning—on her cell.

"What did she say?" he'd ask each time.

And each time Marion would shrug, "Nothing really. We just chatted about what's going on down there and what's happening with Alyssa and Sam's kids. You know...."

"Like nothing has happened? Like we're all still one big happy family?"

"I guess so, Robert. It's delicate territory, you know.

Then right in the middle of their Thanksgiving meal, Robert said, "I'm going down there." (He was certain she would have shown up by now.) But Marion smiled that fake smile he detested and said that was a bad idea. So did Sam, turning away. Alyssa just shook her head and asked him when he was going to learn. So did Garrison, whom he called a disloyal sonofabitch.

And then, shortly before Christmas, about the time when his affair with Brenda Holloway led to Marion finding solace in the pastor's arms, when he and Marion stumbled back to couples therapy, when everything was falling apart around him, Robert finally lost his will. He stopped threatening to go down to Asheville. He stopped calling.

Chapter Seven

After a quick shower and a dreamy breakfast at the hotel café, Marion and Jed folded themselves into the Corolla to make the fifteen-minute drive up the coast to Quepos.

This time Carlos Estrada was in his office, sitting alone behind an enormous, messy, wooden desk, piles of papers on either end, an old-looking Dell desktop and printer right in the center. Over in the corner, a copier whirred, shuffling out sheet after sheet of a flyer for an open house in Jaco, the papers fluttering beneath the languid ceiling fan. Carlos heaved himself up when he saw the two Americans open the glass door and walk in.

"Senora Tevees?"

"Si," she agreed, with that pleasant smile Jed had seen her use so often in social situations. "And this is my friend and partner, Jed Blackstone." She turned to Jed, "Jed, this is Senor Estrada."

Carlos's eyebrows went up as he reached for the tall gringo's hand. "Welcome, both of you. And now, I suppose, you two would like to go see what I think is going to be the perfect new house for you?" He scooped a folder off one of the piles, flipped the switch on the ceiling fan, withdrew a key from his pocket, and said, "I will drive you up there."

"Up there" was, in Senor Estrada's rehearsed words as he drove down the coast, "A beautiful mountain cottage in the hills above Manuel Antonio, where you will be enjoying peace, tranquility, and incredible, unobstructed views of Costa Rica Central Valley and mountains. This property, Senor and Senora, has wonderful manicured gardens and is furnished by interior decorators, creating an incredible ambience mixed with..." he looked down at the sheet in his lap, "an European Provenzal style."

Jed, suddenly lightheaded, had to force himself to say the words: "I'm definitely looking forward to seeing it, Senor Estrada."

"Oh yes," said Marion from the back seat, her hand on Jed's shoulder. "it sounds absolutely wonderful." She glanced right and left at the sea and the jungle, a broad smile materializing on her face.

As Senor Estrada drove his banged up Nissan Altima down the narrow coast road toward Manuel Antonio, Jed kept pressing his right foot to the floorboards trying to slow down the car around the curves. Behind him Marion jabbered on, full of unbridled enthusiasm for the jungle whizzing by, and the new life they were headed into.

A squealing left up a narrow road and a quick right through an open rusting gate brought them into what the previous owners had called Casa Cielo en la Tierra. From the outside, the cottage was everything Estrada had promised: pink and luscious, surrounded by palm fronds, air plants, and orchids, with howler monkeys swinging onto the green tin roof and the kind of valley view that had Marion squealing on the ride down from San Jose. It looked just like the photos Carlos had emailed her a few weeks before. A green lizard scurried away with a throaty roar when they got out of the car.

"Oh my God, that is one beautiful lizard," she cried. "Jed! Can you believe this?"

Estrada was beaming, "Si, si!" he said, extending his arm as if leading royalty down a primrose path.

Jed nodded, put his hands in the pockets of his shorts and, after looking all around at a world he never considered would be his, followed Marion and Carlos into the pink cottage.

———————

Marion absolutely loved the place. The long deck, the view, the kitchen, the painted beams in the living room, the monkeys, the "house iguana," the coconut tree, the vanilla smell of the bedroom. Out on the veranda, she wanted to shriek along with the monkeys swinging through the jungle.

Jed was quiet in the backseat, ponderous it seemed, the entire ride back to Quepos.

An hour later, after filling out some preliminary paperwork and promising to call Estrada the following morning with a bid, Marion drove back to Manuel Antonio, parked the Corolla in front of the hotel, slammed the tinny door shut behind her, and sashayed her way around the hood to Jed, who stood with a closed-lip smile, his big hands in his pockets.

Without a word, she unbuttoned his white linen shirt, her hands sweeping over his smooth hard chest and around and around to the soft love handles over his hips. "Come, let's celebrate our new house, our new life," she said, grabbing his hand and leading him to their room where she closed the door and yanked the belt buckle open, quickly unsnapping and unzipping, her fingers sliding into his underpants.

"Wait," he said.

"Ooh, sweetheart, I don't want to wait." She looked up into his dark eyes and, reaching down between his legs, said, "Doesn't feel like you want to wait either."

"We should talk."

"Oh Jedi-Jedi-Jedi, I'm done talking." Her fingers swirling around, making him close his eyes, "I want to make love with you, I want to buy that beautiful cottage on the hill, I want to walk the beach, I want to learn the songs of these gorgeous birds, I want to chat with the monkeys and the lizards. I don't want to wait one second longer."

"But—"

But even Jed Blackstone had to know how it goes when a woman slides your shorts down to your ankles and kneels before you.

And twenty minutes later, lying in the rumpled bed, the ceiling fan moving the warm air across their sweaty bodies, Marion smiling behind her closed eyes, Jed was the first to break the silence. "You're amazing, Marion, I don't, I can't imagine, how this happened."

"I seduced you."

He laughed out loud then, "I mean, beyond all this...what did happen? How did I, small-town bachelor minister, end up here—in this bed—with the most beautiful woman in the world—in Costa Rica of all places?"

"That's a whole novel, maybe a trilogy, Jedi. But for the time being, let's just agree that the universe wants us here...wants us together. Why else would we be here?"

"Right," he said, sounding perhaps a little sad. "I mean, is it possible that this is all God's will?"

"Of course, Jedi. How could it not be?"

His eyes were pooling. "I've spent years pondering God's will, unable to come up with anything beyond scripture that I can hold on to. And now you say it so simply."

The next morning, when Marion woke to the screeching noises in the jungle, Jed had already gone. Again.

She made some coffee, brought it out to the patio, sat in the plastic chair, stared out into the screeching jungle, and waited. Just like the day before.

This was beginning to feel a little too familiar. "The story of my life," she said to an iguana skittering out from some bushes. "The short story," she added, thinking now about the melancholy boys—and then men—who she always found attractive, the ones who awakened in her a kind of unbound girlish zeal, which always seemed to brighten their serious lives, and which made everything fun and beautiful and even innocent.

Sitting alone on the patio at the edge of the deep forest overlooking the Pacific Ocean, she drew a mental line from the eternally troubled Billy Rogers in high school to ponytailed George Benson's devout existential angst early on in college, to Robert. Robert. *Oh Robert!* How her infectious enthusiasm was tamped down by his bullying nature, first during their unhappy honeymoon in Bermuda, then through the natural weariness brought on by children, then the petty PTA, the condescending jackasses in the Little League, the self-righteous church elders, her aging, whining parents, all of that. And then, of course, there was Robert's affair, leaving only fleeting embers of joy in her darkened spirit.

She looked down the dirt road and remembered how that zeal was re-ignited early on during those long, weepy counseling sessions with the overly sincere new pastor in Elting. How the man who seemed to have all the answers eventually revealed his own dark spirit to her in the awkward homilies emerging out of their intimate conversation. Then, less and less awkwardly, in their springtime walks along the river behind the church.

Chapter Eight

As Robert pulled into the driveway at 398 Warren Wilson Road where Beryl rented an attic apartment, he was still trying out opening lines.

But he hadn't planned on crying when he saw her striding through a swinging screen door, her beautiful long red hair flowing behind like she was a model on some hippie runway.

She had on a pink floral sundress with spaghetti straps, billowing up in the wind, a smile that reminded him of Marion as she skipped his way.

Father and daughter stood five yards apart, suspended in overlapping time, each waiting for the other to breach the chasm. Robert wanted to rush up to her, but was paralyzed.

Eventually, Beryl nodded and, that smile still in place, moved slowly toward her father. "Hi, Dad," she whispered in his ear as she wrapped her thin white arms around his thick neck, his hands still at his sides.

Unable to do anything else, he was sobbing. "I'm sorry," he said and finally finding the strength to lift his arms, hugged her back. "I'm sorry, Beryl, sweetheart, I didn't expect to be so blubbery."

She stepped back out of his embrace and laughed, not cruelly, "I don't think I've ever seen you cry."

He nodded, his cheeks wet.

"It's been a long time, Dad. I'm glad to see you, though."

"Me too," he said reaching for her hand.

"My God, Dad, your hand is all swollen!"

He turned over his hand and looked at it as if noticing for the first time that it was filled with fluid. "Oh this," he said, "it's nothing, just more of the old stuff with me and my friend edema. It's just me being on the road…I'm sure my hands'll be back to their old arthritic skin and bones in another week."

A half hour later, after giving his daughter a tour of his traveling home and telling her bits and pieces, dribs and drabs, of his meeting with Clover and Mountain Eagle—leaving out the magic brownies part—father and daughter sat on the screened porch of the house, a pitcher of sweet tea between them.

"So…" he said, seconds after the conversation hit a lull, the psychoanalytic voice shouldering out the stranger, this new man he was becoming, "should we talk about what happened?"

"No," she said. "No." She reached over and patted his hand, smiling as if she was bringing him into some kind of conspiracy. "Despite what people say, some things are best left unsaid. No profit in spilt milk."

He didn't know what to say. How do people not talk about what happens between them?

Beryl went on, "You know, animals are free of the yoke of self-analysis. They don't go to psychoanalysis to find closure. They don't wear 'hair shirts'. They just move ahead to the next meal."

"But I want you to know—"

"Let me show you my apartment," she said, interrupting his returning paralysis. "Then we'll hop into your super-duper tent, and I'll give you a tour of the campus."

Robert nodded. "I just want to say I'm sorry again."

Beryl looked intently into her father's eyes, lips pressed together. "You already did. And let's just leave it at that. You know Huxley's quote? 'Rolling in the muck is not the best way of getting clean.'"

Which was when Steven Sutherland lumbered out onto the porch in green basketball shorts and a Golden Eagles T-shirt and all hope of talking about what had happened flitted off like a dragonfly.

So, it turned out that it was Stephen Sutherland who'd flinched. Or at least that was Robert's conclusion, one he kept to himself as they walked into the small studio apartment, which was like entering a trapdoor back into the Sixties, a big Indian print bedspread on the one windowless wall, posters of Dylan, Kerouac, Ginsberg, Jerry Garcia in between windows and cabinets and doors, window air conditioner humming. On the bedside table were two framed pictures of Sam and Alyssa and their families.

Robert shrugged before he started talking. "As you probably know, I'm a little in the dark about everything that's gone on. Both of you live here now? I mean, full time?"

Stephen returned the shrug. "Turned out I was desperately unhappy in Milwaukee without Beryl," he said without a hint of the shame Robert expected when a man follows a woman.

"So…?"

Stephen smiled. "So I charmed and finagled and maybe even bullied my way into a January admission to Wake Forest School of Divinity…it's only about two hours from here."

"We'll move to Black Mountain after the term," Beryl said. "Make the commute a little shorter for him." She looked at the tall, lanky man. "It's only two years of classes—and then they said he can do his pastoral internship around here." She rubbed her father's bare, stringy upper arm.

Then she swept her hand around as if she was on stage, graciously imploring the audience to applaud the cast. "So…do you like it?"

"I do," he said, the teariness rising up in him again, "I do…" pushing it down. "After my ride on the Magic Bus with Mountain and Clover, though, I have to say it feels a bit like déjà vu all over again."

Beryl cocked her head to the side. "Déjà vu is all over again, Dad. And don't confuse all this with some pot-smoking hippies. I teach a lot of them, you know—and that's not what this is all about."

"I was just—" he started, then pulled back: "Sorry…just making a bad joke."

She shrugged.

"I guess I'm still nervous. So…," he said, reaching into his pocket, "before we head out, I have something for you. Actually, two things."

Beryl drew in a long quiet breath and held it in her lungs waiting for her father to extract his hand from his pocket.

"Your hand!" she gasped when she saw the swollen paw.

Robert held up his palm. "Nothing to worry about, I've got everything under control. I just need to get a prescription filled for a diuretic."

Beryl suddenly seemed annoyed. And Robert was just plain flustered. "But more to the point," he said quickly.

"More to what point?" Beryl asked, not kindly now.

"More to the point about what I was going to say," he said, his tongue beginning to clog his airway, coughing, coughing, "I have something I want to give you…something a little odd, but something I think you'd appreciate more than the engagement ring I gave to your sister—and the wedding band I gave to your brother."

"Yeah," she said backing up one step, the old anger rising behind her eyes, "I guess I'm intrigued…but what the hell is it, if it's not gold or diamond? Your old high school ring?"

His fist remained clenched around the gift. "I apologize for being so mysterious about all this, but bear with me…I guess this all started when your mom returned her engagement ring to me. She said that since it was originally my mother's she thought it should stay in the family. I didn't want it, but she insisted, so I gave it to Alyssa. I wanted her to know that I loved your mother with all my heart when we got married and, despite my personal failures," he looked over at his frowning daughter, "I loved her for a long, long time afterward."

When Beryl didn't say anything, he went on: "And then it occurred to me that I should give my wedding ring to your brother so, despite everything that happened, he would know that she once loved me with all her heart as well."

"Okay," came a small voice from the less-anguished past, "so... where do I come in? What's left for me?"

"So...," he opened his fist, and there in his fleshy palm was a silver necklace and a small gift box. "This is easy," he said, picking up the necklace with that thick thumb and forefinger and extending it her way, "and I'll explain all about it in a minute."

Beryl gently lifted the necklace off his finger and held it in her palm, an unsure, childlike smile appearing on her freckled face.

"Now this," he said just above a whisper, the gift box in his open palm, his upper lip quivering. "Well, first, I want to apologize in advance if this speech seems a little canned, but I've been talking to myself for days on end, rehearsing what I wanted to say to you."

Stephen interrupted then, asking whether he should leave them alone, but neither Robert nor Beryl seemed to have heard him. Beryl, who appeared to grow ever more diminutive in that hushed moment, stared deeply into her father's watery eyes.

Robert cleared the phlegm from his throat. "Beryl, sweetheart, I wanted you to know that you were chosen out of the boundless love between your mother and me."

It was soon obvious that she had no idea what he was talking about. Stephen also looked confused.

He inhaled deeply through his nose. "Well, the short version is…that the pregnancies that brought us Sam and Alyssa, while greeted with pleasure and gratitude, were wholly unplanned, except in the sense that we knew we wanted to have kids at some time."

He nodded. She nodded back, her eyes glistening.

"You, on the other hand, were in our most pure and loving thoughts when Mom went off the pill." He held up the box and opened it, folding back the pink tissue paper to reveal a brass key attached to a black, oval plastic tag. "We were at the Nauset Knoll Lodge on Cape Cod. And you were in our thoughts when we made love and you were conceived—"

"Whoa!" she sputtered and held up her hand.

He paused, wide-eyed.

"Too much information for me, Dad," she said quickly. "We're just getting to know each other again." But now her eyes were pooling.

"Frankly, I didn't know why at the time I kept this thing," he continued. "I just put it in my pocket when we left the motel that one morning, carried it around with me all that day—and then brought it to the office with me the next day. I remember thinking that I should drop it in the mail. But I just couldn't bring myself to drive over to the post office, so I put it in my desk."

Lightheaded now, he lowered himself down on the bed. "I discovered it in a corner of my desk when I was clearing out the office. So I put it in a box and brought it to you…to do whatever you want with it. I know it isn't a diamond or gold, and it's not worth any money, but as I've come to realize—far too late it seems—love is more precious than anything. And I am hoping that this key is a reminder of just how much hope and love courses through your veins."

Her palm was open without her knowing it, and Robert gently

laid the key in her hand, and when she leaned across to give him a kiss, he kissed her cheek.

"I don't know what to say," she finally said. She held her open palm out to Stephen. He attempted a smile. "It's pretty damn weird, Dad...and it's kind of beautiful." She giggled nervously then. "Pretty fucking damn weird. I don't know what to say."

"You don't have to say anything. I know it's a strange gift, but I just hope you'll keep it somewhere and sometimes think about what it means."

She nodded, sucking in her lower lip, anxious to move along to something else. "And this...?" picking up the necklace.

"Oh that," as if he'd forgotten, "that is a necklace my old pal Garrison and I made a long time ago in Madison, one of a pair actually, a few years before I met your mom, before I had any thoughts of being a psychologist, before I had anything anyone might identify as a thought inside my head. Somewhere along the way I lost my necklace; Garrison gave me his when we said good-bye."

She raised her eyebrows, her glistening eyes shifting toward her boyfriend. He just shrugged.

"I don't know why I want you to have this, except maybe to show you that I wasn't always so serious, I wasn't always such a know-it-all." He shrugged. "I just want you to have it. I came to give you the key; I just want you to have this."

In one fluid motion, Beryl lifted it from his outstretched palm, slid the chain over her head and, beaming, did a kind of plié in Stephen's direction. Stephen applauded, leaning in, trying to decipher the hieroglyphics.

"S-H-I-T," said Robert.

"Oh?"

"S-H-I-T...the letters twisted around and laid on top of each other. Can you see them?"

"Oooh," Stephen nodded again, still blank-faced.

Beryl picked the pendant off her chest. "Oh I see...I see!" and she burst out in that deep laughter he hadn't heard since she was in high school. "This is maybe the stupidest thing I have ever seen, Dad. This is incredibly lame...totally Hunter Thompson together with that bizarre motel key—a brand new kind of fear and loathing...in Asheville."

She glanced back at her father to see if he was insulted.

He was. Sort of. And sort of not. In any case, now it was done. He didn't know what he expected. "Yup, pretty lame," he repeated. "But that's pretty much what I wanted you to have—and know."

Beryl leaned down again and kissed her father on his cheek. "This is very cool," she said, but when he tilted his head like he always did when he thought he was the hippest cat in the universe, she added, "Not the pendant—this is about as dumbass as it gets—but that you're giving it to me, that's actually the cool part."

Inflated as quickly as he was deflated, Robert managed to stand up and, abandoning any pretense that Stephen was in the room, wrapped his bear-like arms around his daughter's bony shoulders, tears again flowing down his unshaven cheeks, inhaling the scent from her hair just as he did when she was an infant.

She wrestled herself away, saying, "Okay, so...I think I'm going to wear this silver SHIT as a talisman." Then she waited until his eyes met hers, "But you should know that the jury is still out about that key thing." She shivered. "Not a vision I want to keep inside my head." She held up the key, then put it back in the box, folded the tissue paper over it, replaced the lid, and laid it down on the table.

Robert nodded again, more gravely now, in the clarity of the moment, deeply saddened that the inspired gesture proved so un-inspirational.

"Dad, get a grip. I'm not going to throw it out. I know what you're aiming for, it's just…just a little bit weird, you know."

"I know."

"Then we're okay?"

He nodded.

"Good."

She picked up the box again, walked over to the oak bureau, opened the top drawer, and dropped it in.

Chapter Nine

The negotiations were as easy and friendly as the country itself. The asking price for the mountainside cottage was $200,000. Marion, whose money it was, was paying with funds from the divorce settlement, offered $150,000. Despite Jed's insistent suggestion that she get the best price, Marion was determined not to outduel the seller, so she and the Castros met right in the middle, at $175,000. *Eso fue fácil* she thought, as pleased with her financial acumen as with her emerging comfort with Spanish.

The following morning, as they were driving off to Senor Estrada's office in Quepos to sign the papers, Marion singing happily along with some salsa station, Jed reached over and flipped off the radio. He waited until she glanced his way. "I'm not sure I can go through with this," he said.

"Don't be silly, Jedi, of course you can." She braked for a lizard scooting across the rutted road.

"I can, Mari, I know I can, but I don't know at what cost to my soul. 'Where could I go from Thy Spirit, and where could I flee from Thy Face?'"

"Oh my lord, Jed, don't be so damn dramatic. We've been through all this before. We're in love. We have a lot to atone for, but that—"

"Marion, I think you've forgotten that I was—I am—a minister. That's from one of the Psalms, 139."

She pulled the Corolla off to the side of the rutted road, put the shift into neutral, and pulled up the parking brake. She spoke into the dusty windshield: "I know where it comes from, Jed Blackstone. Perhaps you have forgotten that I was your congregant."

He sighed. "I have not forgotten who you are, Marion."

"Then I have definitely not forgotten that you are a man of the cloth, dear Jed." She continued to stare straight ahead, both hands gripping the wheel. "Even if I ever wanted to, I know who you are, perhaps better than you know yourself. And I certainly love you more completely, despite your evident failings, than you do yourself."

He put his hand on her bare smooth knee. "I know you do, I know you do, but I'm being torn apart by my love for you, Mari." He looked her way now, his eyes filling. "I'm sorry. I'm so sorry. I just don't know how to live this life that we're about to create down here. It feels so right…and so wrong and—"

She blew out the breath. "And?"

"And…," he brought his hands together over his chest, "and I think I could live more easily with myself, with my God, with my calling without this—without you—than if I had my heart's desire…this…," he swept his hand across the windshield, "and you. Mari, I love you, I yearn for you, I ache for you. I love you maybe even more than life itself, but these last few days with Pastor Henriquez, I have prayed, I have wept nakedly in His presence begging for direction, and no matter which way I turn, I now understand that I cannot abide such selfishness in myself. I cannot turn away from God. I have a calling and I can't turn and I can't stop hearing it."

"Did it ever occur to you that this is a turn toward God? Naked and weak in His presence, asking for mercy?"

"That sounds like a sinner's rationalization, Mari."

Marion nodded, swallowed the words she yearned to say, nodded again, signaled to get back on the road even though no one was coming, and continued on the potholed way toward Quepos. She flipped the radio back on, salsa filling the empty spaces.

"Do you understand what I'm saying?" he said finally over the insistent beat.

Marion didn't flinch, didn't acknowledge the question, didn't seem to know there was anyone in the car but her.

"Mari, please just listen to me for a moment." He turned down the radio until it was just a buzz. "I know that I may sound like one of those self-absorbed navel watchers that we always laugh about, but I know now what sacrifice really is about."

At Senor Estrada's office, she skidded to a stop and, as if she was talking to one of her kids, told Jed Blackstone to wait in the car for her.

"Marion, wait, " he said, his hand on her forearm.

"I'll be right back."

"You don't have to cancel the deal."

She looked at him from beneath knitted brows. "I don't have to do anything, Jed. After all this, I have learned that I...I don't have to do anything." When he didn't reply, she told him again to wait in the car. She might as well have added, "Think about what you've done," like some disappointed and disgusted mother.

Jed did as he was told. And fifteen minutes later, after explaining and re-explaining to Senor Estrada and the lawyer, a Senor Cantillos, in progressively moderated tones that she would be putting the house in her name alone, the confused realtor opened the manila folder on his cluttered desk. Marion then signed the papers, wrote a check for $174,529—approximately her share of the house in Elting—and waited patiently for the agent to reach into the drawer and pull out the keys to her new home in the steep hills outside Manuel Antonio.

When they arrived back at the Hotel La Colina, Marion finally broke the tense silence. She said in the most matter-of-fact tone she could muster, "Jed, you should call the airlines and find out when I should drive you back up to San Jose."

He sat back in the seat and pressed his lips together.

When he finally spoke, it was not the tearful reconciliation or the tight-lipped agreement she was expecting. He said, "I'm not leaving, Marion."

"No?"

"I have been invited by Pastor Henriquez to assist him down here, to find my way back to the path."

"Oh?"

"I don't think I can go back to Elting."

Her eyes widened. "Oh…oh, oh Jedi, now I see."

"What do you see, Mari?" he said, his voice full of hope.

"I see now that you're a coward, Jedi. Of all things. I didn't think you were a coward."

He smiled the smile of pastoral self-assurance, "I am not a coward, Mari." His voice was full of the confident resonance of the pulpit that had seduced her so long ago. "I am a lot of things, but I am not a coward. I'm a sinner, Mari—I am a sinner and this is where God has led me to pay my penance."

Marion sat there sweating behind the driver's wheel, her chest heaving up and down as she tried to locate her voice among the ruins of her new life. She could not stem the flow of tears. She looked over, finally: "You are a damned coward, Jed Blackstone."

———————

It was a good thing that furniture was included in the sale of the house, Marion thought, letting herself fall back into the rattan couch and looking around at her new bright floral life— all alone on the Pacific coast of Costa Rica, not a soul to call her own. "How the flying fuck did I end up here in the middle of the jungle at fifty-eight?" she said out loud.

It was a rhetorical question. She knew that. An absurd question. She knew that as well. She knew. "I know I know I know...," she said out loud again. Then, "I better stop talking to myself or..."

Or what? She stood up then, to wander around the empty cottage, into the two sparsely furnished bedrooms, one and a half baths, vast porch overlooking the valley—monkeys swinging through the trees, iguanas under the deck—and then get back in the car again to buy some food for dinner—and, yes, yes, yes finally(!) figure out the rest of her life.

She drove slowly back toward Quepos to the only supermercado she knew—the one on the right, the one with the uniformed policeman standing near the entrance, a machine gun of some sort in his hands, a friendly smile on his broad face. She parked, locked the car, unlocked it, and walked past the armed guard and two smiling men in hats. "Buenos dias," one of them said, holding the brim of his NY Yankees cap, a gaping black hole between bright white incisors, pink tongue poking through.

Walking down the dusty *el pasillos*, she practiced her Spanish as she picked up each item: *el arroz*—rice, los cereals—cereals, el fideo—pasta, las galletas—cookies, la leche—milk, huevos— eggs, las sardinas, vino, agua...and, as when she skipped down Bascomb Hill after acing the Spanish I final at Wisconsin, she strode confidently up to the checkout counter, where she paid 4500 *colons*, held out her hand for *el vuelto* and carried her plastic *bolsos* back to the Corolla.

It was a fleeting pleasure, ending most abruptly when, arms full of groceries, she opened the passenger door and saw Jed's wallet on the floor. She dropped the bags and looked all around the parking lot, not even sure what she was looking for. "Fuck!" she cried. "Fuck fuck fuck!"

Now she would have to track down what's-his-name—Pastor Henriquez?—and, worse, see Jed again while it was all so raw.

And do it all before Jed showed up at her doorstep with that puppy dog look of his. All she wanted to do now was smack him with the back of her hand—for this ("So like him!" she muttered) and everything else.

"Okay," she said, as she loaded the groceries into the trunk, with two wide-eyed locals on the sidewalk watching the white woman yelling at no one. "Okay. I got it. You don't have to hit me over the head with a two by four, I got it. I definitely got it. Oh, did I ever get it!"

And with her overflowing bile spewed out into the humid Costa Rican air, men leaning on the walls of the supermercado with smiles on their faces, Marion got in the driver's seat, turned the ignition, raced the engine, ground the gear into reverse, backed up, jammed the shifter into first, popped the clutch, and skidded back to her new cottage in the deep green jungle to pack away a week's worth of groceries and soothe her aching soul with a cool gin and tonic on the veranda.

When the spitting wires in her brain had untangled themselves enough to allow her to think clearly again, Marion put the wallet in her pocket and walked down toward the beach, where she turned her back on the ocean and looked up at the hills.

All she had to go on was Jed's description of seeing the white cross from the beach near Manuel Antonio.

Chapter Ten

Robert soon realized that leaving Beryl was not nearly as wrenching as reuniting with her. Not that it had been an easy day or all was forgiven, what with her obviously slipping and skidding on all that spilled milk, as she had called it, while they walked around the beautiful campus, and what with Robert intent on not criticizing anything in his daughter's new life, careful, so careful, not to offer any suggestions or assessments about anything, admiring everything she showed him, showering her with saccharine-tasting compliments about her unremarkable office, the brand new gym complex, the views of the Blue Ridge, the giddy students who stooped over their table at the Union cafeteria.

Dinner at the Laughing Seed Café in Asheville was a bit subdued, as lacking in flavor and emotion as the Harmony Bowl, Robert ordered (organic brown rice, organic black beans, grilled organic tofu, steamed organic vegetables, natural sesame ginger sauce) to try to impress his unimpressed daughter.

So everyone—Beryl, Stephen, Robert—was understandably beat by the time they got back to the apartment early that evening, yawning, yawning, making quick arrangements to have breakfast together in Asheville before Robert headed out the next morning.

And after a sleepless night for both father and daughter, the next morning the three of them were finally done with what Robert was privately calling "The Passion Play." Standing outside the Tupelo Honey restaurant in downtown Asheville, he shook hands with Stephen Sutherland, patting him on the shoulder as if he really liked the guy, then turned to Beryl, hunching down over her and clasping her in his arms, tightly, tightly, too tightly, holding his little girl, his old pal, knowing he might never hold her again.

Beryl returned the hug, but Robert could tell she was relieved to finally push back out of his embrace, to watch him flash a goofy V sign with his fingers and then haul himself up into the captain's chair of the Winnebago, toot the stupid Dukes of Hazzard horn, and wave as he drove off down College Street, the dam of tears bursting behind his dark eyes.

In the sideview mirror, Robert could see Beryl bury herself in Stephen's chest. He drove to the light, then lost them as he made a right turn and one-two-three blocks later pulled over to the curb because he had no idea where he was headed.

Frankly, there was nowhere he wanted to go in Asheville. No one he wanted to see there. Everyone had always told him and Marion that if they ever got to Asheville, they had to see the Biltmore Estate. Back in Elting, when he was plotting out his odyssey, Robert thought it might be fun or interesting or something to spend the day at the Biltmore, but that seemed lame now. Why waste time and money on some wealthy narcissist's quest for vindictive triumph over the universe? There was nothing to do except to get back on the road.

So Robert pulled into the Mobil station on Broadway and filled up the tank, figuring that one tank would take him all the way to where he needed to go. Despite decades of warning his depressed and anxious clients against "magical thinking," Dr. Tevis just knew that his destination would simply appear off the interstate.

Somewhere on I-85 south of Atlanta, the Winnebago on cruise control at a smooth 73 miles an hour, Robert saw the gas warning light go on and a mile later spied a giant Wal-Mart sign over the Jonesboro exit. That was the sign.

He veered across two lanes to get off the highway. It was time. Finally. All his business was taken care of, Robert Tevis was finally free.

A few minutes later, already out of breath and his heart thudding like a water pump behind his barrel chest, Robert leaned into the oversized grocery cart, driving it down the wide aisles like a modern-day Sisyphus pushing his boulder past toys, sheets and towels, propane cylinders, bungee cords, kitchenware until he arrived at Plumbing Supplies, ending in a few choppy steps right in front of a bin of flexible tubing. He reached into his shirt pocket for the scrap of paper on which he'd written "3 inches wide…12 feet long."

"Oh!" he gasped, out loud, amazed that exactly what he was looking for was right in front of him. He reached for the tubing, grasping it with the thick fingers of his left hand before dropping it, shafts of an internal electricity sending spasms up his arm.

He stood there rubbing his tingling hand, running his fingers up and down his arm.

It was then, only then, that Robert decided not to kill himself. He abandoned the cart in the aisle and ran, scurrying past the lines of shoppers behind the registers and out the automatic glass doors, hauling himself up into the RV, his chest heaving, barely allowing himself a deep clean breath before driving out of the parking lot and over to the Sunoco station, filling the gas tank, cranking up the iPod, and merging back into traffic on I-85, nowhere to go, nowhere to stay. Foot steady on the gas pedal, his mind lost in overdrive.

An hour or two later, signs telling him he was approaching Montgomery, Alabama, Robert caught his breath and allowed himself finally to reflect on what had actually happened in the Wal-Mart.

It would have been nice, he thought, if images of Beryl, Alyssa, and Sam had come to him at the moment he touched the tubing—or if he'd heard the voices of his grandchildren—but it was nothing like that. It was pure electricity coursing up and down his arm, and it came from his belly.

"I'm a coward," he said out loud. "I am a goddamn coward." And he pulled off the interstate and, seeing the big sign coming up, drove into the dark corner of yet another Wal-Mart parking lot.

He killed the engine and sat there behind the wheel, staring out the buggy windshield.

In the cold and dark shadows of the closed mega-store, Robert thought back to the moment when Marion passed her engagement ring over the threshold, and how everything seemed ordained from then on—how he would give the rings to Sam and Alyssa and clear his conscience about the affair with Brenda Holloway; how he would say good-bye to Garrison, his only true friend in the world; how he would drive down to Asheville and, after making amends with Beryl and handing her the most bizarre of gifts, he would head off, finally free of all entanglements. The truest thing he had ever done.

Up to the moment that he dropped the tubing in sudden fright, Robert had never been scared, never repulsed, by the notion of doing away with himself. *Putting myself to sleep,* he had thought, like the way they had put their beloved Sadie the black Lab to sleep. After all, the damn disease was going to kill him anyway. And, as a member of the Hemlock Society back in Elting, something that had always irked Marion in the extreme, he had imagined it as a principled act.

The original plan, if anyone could call it a plan, was to leave Asheville, drive five or six hours, get off the highway somewhere between Atlanta, Georgia, and Montgomery, Alabama, drive down progressively narrow country roads, deep deep deep into some imagined southern pine-studded wilderness, and stopping near a bucolic stream or pond, find the rolling meadow of his dreams. Then he would hook up the 3-inch, 12-foot length of flexible tubing to the exhaust pipe, pass it up through the sliding window, turn on the engine, and, picking up Proust for the last time, fall into eternal rest.

Well, that had been the plan.

What he hadn't planned on was the shock as he touched the tubing. Was it repulsion? Remorse? Fright?

"I am a miserable coward," he repeated, still shocked at how little he understood about himself—how much of a danger he was to himself. Yet, sitting in the warm captain's chair of the quiet Winnebago, Robert was strangely exhilarated, giggling, in the face of his own unintended defiance, a boy who had shoplifted death from itself.

Giggling! Me!

Moments later, Robert hauled himself up out of the captain's chair and walked back to the "kitchen" to locate the last can of Dinty Moore in the tiny cupboard. He warmed the stew, poured it into a plastic bowl, spread some butter on an end piece of white bread, and sat down at the small table. He ate all of it, sopping up the last of it with the bread, in the silence of the dimly lit Winnebago, Robert looked out the window at the stark shadows of the empty parking lot and shook his head at his foolish life, a sad smile creeping across his face.

He stood then, washed the pot, bowl and silverware, and side-stepped back up to the front of the vehicle. Dropping his bulk on the driver's seat, Robert poked at the iPod several times, turned the ignition and when the song came on sang along with Son Volt, "…two hands on the wheel, both feet on the floor," as he exited the parking lot and merged back onto the highway. With nowhere special to go, and no resolve to change direction, Robert

Tevis barreled his lonely way southward, toward the delta, New Orleans, wondering if that battered and torn city would show him mercy or at least a way to live in the world again. Though he was sure it was mercy that he needed right then.

Two days later, sitting alone at a picnic table at the Parkway Grill in mid-city New Orleans, the coleslaw juice from an oyster po' boy running down his stubbled chin, his shaggy hair grown over his collar, Robert tried to figure out what had happened back at the Wal-Mart. Why he was suddenly so frightened of ending his misery, a whole life in ruins, a merciful mercy killing, like he'd once thought was his fate.

He wondered how killing oneself made perfect sense one day and how choosing life made even more sense a few days later. He shook his head with the understanding that nothing made sense anymore, that understanding was futile, a deplorable admission from a man who had been a practicing psychotherapist for the last thirty-five years, a man who prided himself in asking the hard questions of his clients.

What he did know was this: He had never known such sadness as he'd felt hugging Beryl, saying that long good-bye in Asheville, his fingers in the spaces between her ribs. A deep, undulating, enduring sadness from which he'd instantly known, her thin arms around his waist, that there would be no escape.

He forced himself to remember how he had sobbed like a child all the way to the Jonesboro Wal-Mart, crying first for his lost child, then his missing grandchildren, then his broken marriage, his whole botched life, the sum of everything gone horribly wrong.

Everything gone horribly wrong, and there was Alannis Morissette and her squeaky voice crackling through the speakers at the Parkway Grill, "Well life has a funny way of sneaking up on you / When you think everything's okay and everything's going right / And life has a funny way of helping you out when / You think everything's gone wrong / and everything blows up / In your face."

He grimaced at the irony. Everything had blown up, right in his face, and yet there he was still alive, Robert Tevis, PhD, sitting at a sticky picnic table in New Orleans. He had decided to live.

Or maybe he had just decided not to die.

Or maybe he hadn't decided anything at all.

Robert wiped his chin with a paper towel and looked at his hand. Now what the hell was he going to do?

Chapter Eleven

A pretty woman, forties maybe, edging up on fifty, a tray in her hands, long brown hair making her appear younger than the crow-foot eyes revealed, leaned over and nudged him with her elbow, "Anybody sittin' there?"

He glanced up, mouth open, somewhat surprised that he was not invisible, and, nodding in greeting, moved himself and his tray down the picnic table.

She sat, picked up her shrimp po'boy and a Diet Coke, and used her elbow to push away the empty tray. "Name?" she said.

"Name?"

"Yeah, your name. I figure if we're gonna eat together I should know your name."

"Robert," he said. He did not feel friendly.

"Okay, Bob, nice to meet you and thanks for sharing your table. I got a few questions for you."

He ignored her. Reached for his oyster po'boy.

"Jesus, that hand is swollen! You hit something?"

He sighed. "No. Just need some medication. What's the question?"

She looked confused. "Oh, sorry—I guess I got distracted by that mitt you're wearing."

He glared at her and returned to his sandwich.

"So, this is how it's going to go…" She picked up the po'boy and bit off a big chunk. "I'm Jen Magruder, itinerant food writer, nice to meetcha and all that. Now you're gonna tell me what ya think of that juicy po'boy and I'll drop your name in my next review."

Robert shrugged, "It's good, I guess."

"Aw crap, Bob, you're gonna make me work for this, right? Is that your deal, you're withholding?"

"What?" He felt the old anger, the lost anger, rise in his chest. Who the hell was this rude woman? "I'm not withholding," he said. "I'm just eating. But I'd have to say you're pretty damn arrogant."

She smirked. "Yeah, probably—gets me in some trouble sometimes, but sometimes it's the only way into a good story. So, Bob, why you suddenly hidin' your hands like that?"

"I think we're done talking, Ms. Magruder." He lifted the sandwich to his mouth and held it there.

"Deal," she said, "but first I'm gonna tell you that you look like a man who's been to hell and back—and," she tilted her head to accompany the smirk, "I have to admit there's something attractive about that. My downfall. Then I'm gonna tell you that I think you're pretty damn hot for an old guy...what? Fifty-fve? Fifty-six? Fifty-seven-years-old?" She nodded like she was looking at cattle.

He smiled then, unduly flattered, so easily turned around. "Sixty and frankly not feeling so hot. You, on the other hand..." He didn't finish. His words had abandoned him.

Jen Magruder smiled knowingly. "Thanks, but don't think you'll be getting in my shorts any time soon, Bobby. I'm just telling it like it is. Gives life and food a little spice, a little McIlhennys, y'know? So, you live around here?"

He twisted around and pointed toward the Winnebago.

"Those ugly apartments?"

He laughed, still a bit giddy from the flattery. "No, not the apartments, that Winnebago over there."

"Very interesting," she said nodding and wiping her mouth with the back of her hand. "You don't look the type." She leaned back then, scrunched up her thin lips, and surveyed the man across the table. "Hmmm, longish hair, two-week growth of beard, good teeth, and you don't stink. Hmmm, I'd say a professor or...maybe an architect?"

Still flattered, he gestured for her to keep guessing.

"Bob, Bob, Bob, no games—I'm done guessing."

"But you're the one who started it." He suddenly felt like a college freshman at the Pub in Madison, jousting with some girl with far better skills than he ever had back then.

She raised her eyebrows and glared at him as if he was an obstinate child. "What do you do, Bob?"

"Shrink," he said, even though he hated the term, had often scowled at his wife and kids when they called him a head shrinker.

"Right—shoulda known." One more bite. And with her mouth full, she said, "Hands?"

Robert was going to object, but he couldn't quite figure out what he was protecting. "It's the CHF."

"Never heard of it."

"Congestive Heart Failure."

"Sounds serious."

He shrugged. "The 'failure' part makes it sound worse than it is. I'm controlling it with diet and medication, ACE Inhibitors."

She waved her long fingers over her head. "Whoa...right over my head, Bobby. You gonna be all right?"

He was biting his lower lip now. "I think so. I've just got to get the refill. I've been on the road."

"Good." She flashed a broad smile. "Now that we got that outta the way, you like that po'boy?"

"Actually, I do. In fact, it's probably as good as anything I've ever tasted. I know that sounds stupid, but..." He stopped before saying something adolescent like "The first day of the rest of my life."

"Not at all, Bobby, this is looking like the best shrimp po' boy in the South—and I'm a bit of an expert."

He looked over at her now. She was beautiful. The kind of high cheekbone, low-living beautiful he read about in James Lee Burke novels. He must've been smiling.

"You want to sleep with me?"

"What?"

"You heard me."

"Well," now he knew he was smiling, a big goofy grin he hadn't worn since those lost college days, "you, you caught me off guard, I frankly don't know what to say…"

"Just answer the question."

"Yeah, I guess." He rubbed his nose.

"Thought so." She laid her hand on his forearm. "Keep your pants on, Dr. Phil, I was just making sure we're on the same page."

An hour later, they were walking along Bayou St. John and he had already told her the whole story—or at least the parts of the story he thought would not make her leave—about his marriage, his affair, his kids, the sale of the house, the drive to Asheville. He left out the motel key and the SHIT necklace. He left out the aborted suicide story. He skipped over the fact that he was told by Dr. Verilli never to eat fried foods again.

"What's your story?" he finally asked.

"I was wonderin' when you were gonna get around to that. I don't guess you were a very good shrink."

He laughed, maybe his first big belly laugh in a few weeks if you don't count getting blitzo high with the kids in the Wal-Mart parking lot, which of course he didn't really remember. "I used to think I was pretty good, but I've recently come around to thinking otherwise."

"Aw, don't be so hard on yourself, Bobby." She bumped him

with her shoulder and then slipped her hand through his arm.

"So...," he said already grinning, "what brings you here today? How can I help you?"

"Well," she said, leaning into him, "you definitely can't help me anymore than I can help you."

Robert clamped her elbow into his ribs and stopped walking, his now-shaggy hair blowing in the warm wind. He looked intently at this very odd and oddly beautiful woman whose dark eyes just met his: "Of all the gin joints in all the towns in all the world, she walks into mine."

"Louis," she said without a moment's pause, "I think this is the beginning of a beautiful friendship."

Turned out Jen Magruder was in New Orleans on a paid mission to find the best po'boys in the Deep South. Originally from Albany, New York, she was what she called "a freelance low-rent food writer" who had once "prep-cooked, sous-cheffed, and basically coked up my way from Poughkeepsie to Pomona." She then went to the CIA to get legit but found she hated how women were treated in big kitchens. "So I hooked on with the Food Network, did some contract work for Martha Stewart's rag, and then went out on my own."

She was working right then for *The Picnic Table*, a publication designed for Costco, Wal-Mart, and Target customers. "I'm going big time again, though, Bobby...got a call from some fey bozo at the Wash Post LifeStyle Section who heard I was working on the po'boy trail and thought his readers might like some 'down home' cuisine and would I blah blah blah.

"Turns out that those folks inside the Beltway want to get their manicured paws dirty on an occasional Saturday night. Slum Suckers, I call 'em." She patted his belly. "Sort of exactly what you were doing over at the Parkway. Am I right, Dr. Tevis?"

"No…" he laughed, offended.

"I am right."

"No no no…"

She sneered. "Haute cuisine is written all over you, Bobby, all that high falutin' New York bullshit is sweatin' like truth right out of your pores. You were slum suckin', right?"

"No!" he said, insulted. "Really. I just heard that the best food in New Orleans could be found at Mother's down in the Warehouse District and up here at the Parkway Diner. That's the truth."

"Who told you?"

He looked embarrassed.

"C'mon," she coaxed.

"No one," he admitted, following his brand spanking new promise, made behind the wheel at the last Wal-Mart parking lot, to tell the truth, no matter what. "Well, I guess I read it in my *Lonely Planet* book. It said it would be a shame to visit New Orleans, go to all the fancy restaurants like Commanders and Emerils and Galatois…and actually 'miss out on the finest cuisine in the whole damn city.' That may be a direct quote."

She slid her arm out of the crook of his elbow, swiveled around, took his face in both hands and kissed him right on the lips. A long soft kiss. "I wrote that," she said.

When their lips parted and Robert opened his eyes, Jen Magruder still had his unshaven cheeks in her hands. No smirk on her beautiful lined face. "Now that was not too shabby, Bobby."

He was speechless, nodding as she continued to hold him in place. "I'll tell you what," she said and let her hands fall away from his face, reaching into the back pocket of her cargo shorts, "I have some work to do, but this here's my card. Let's meet someplace for dinner."

"Mother's?" he said too quickly.

"No. I'm thinkin' Liuza's."

"Where's that?"

"Call me later, Robert, " she sang, with a little toodle-loo wave over her shoulder as she walked over to Esplanade.

Robert looked around at the bayou—abandoned kayaks in the grass, newly gentrified shotguns on either side—not sure how to get back to the Parkway Diner or the Winnebago. He checked his cell—no messages, no missed calls—the reality of his new life just then sinking in: Not a soul on earth knew or cared where he was.

It was 1:30. Heading back in the direction he and Jen had walked, Robert punched in 411 on his cell phone and, a little out of breath, asked for the number of a Jesse Salenger in New Orleans.

Jesse had been his grad school roommate in a two-bedroom first floor apartment on Rosemary Street in Chapel Hill. Jesse was a year ahead of Robert in the clinical psych program and was in the process of breaking up with his girlfriend when Robert pulled up to the curb .

The girlfriend was Marion. She had transferred to Chapel Hill from Madison that summer because the field biologists were doing such interesting and important studies with red wolves in eastern North Carolina—the kind of work she'd always dreamed of doing. Also, they weren't torturing chimpanzees like that SOB Harlow was doing in his world-famous monkey labs.

Marion was loading her white VW bug as he pulled up in his rusty Dodge Dart. In the soon-to-be-lost vernacular of the time, she was a dish, a babe. Robert couldn't stop staring at her—those high cheekbones, that swoop of her ass, those gorgeous, shapely, smooth calves. She shook his hand and said "Maybe you'll get along better with him than I did."

Robert nodded and smiled at the girl who didn't say good-bye to Jesse before sliding into the VW and roaring off. Which would have been the beginning and end of their connection—no reason to know they'd been in Madison around the same time—if Robert hadn't happened to see Marion the next day at the Hardback Cafe on Columbia Street. A nod, a shy smile, a tentative hand in the air when she left.

A few days later, he ran into her again near The Well on campus for a couple of foot-shuffling moments of instantly unforgettable conversation. And then, because he was already stumbling into love with her, Robert just happened to meander by The Well every day at the same time, hoping to see her again...and get her phone number...and marry her.

The whole thing could have—should have—been terribly awkward with Jesse, especially after Robert did manage to get Marion's number a few days later, at The Well, of course—and more especially after Marion moved in with Robert right after Thanksgiving, a thin Sheetrock wall between them and her former lover.

But Jesse was apparently unperturbed, already having moved on to a fun-loving undergraduate named Teasha from Asheville—and then to beautiful but bedraggled Misty from Four Oaks. He shrugged, "No skin off my back, buddy—I was glad to see her go. Too many demands. If you can make a go of it, all the more power to you."

"Yeah?" Robert said, meaning *You really don't mind me humping your former girlfriend?*

"Oh yeah, although I probably should warn you that she can be a real ball buster...if you don't mind me saying so. But you seem a little more copasetic than me, so..." he smirked, "rock on, bro," raising his fist in the air like the jackass he always was.

And that was that.

Or that would have been that except Marion had one demand right after they returned from Thanksgiving break. She dropped her suitcase on the filthy rug, looked around at the dirty plates on the coffee table, the beer cans on the television, a Trojan wrapper on the arm of the sofa, and said, "I just can't live under the same roof as that asshole."

So Robert and Marion found another apartment out on Airport Road and moved in together the next weekend. And a few days before Christmas, soon after she told Robert she was pregnant, he waited until she had left for classes and called his mother to tell her he was going to ask Marion to marry him.

When he got home for Christmas, his mother gave him her engagement ring. "Take this," she said.

He refused, but she insisted.

Chapter Twelve

Marion parked by the beach at Manuel Antonio, and walked down the rough concrete steps to the sand and then to the edge of the azure blue water. There was no one around. "So this is where you find yourself," she said out loud, hands on hips, "when you are all alone in the universe."

It was a statement, not a question, and she uttered it without an intended listener, not even herself, and certainly not God, just casting it out to the uncaring waves and empty, enduring cosmos. For a few desolate moments she considered pulling a Virginia Woolf—a phrase she remembered out of those long past college days in Chapel Hill—simply walking into the water until it was over her head, then inviting the warm waters into her lungs.

It would serve him right, she thought, that spineless soldier for Christ. It would serve all of them right, everyone who judged her so harshly. Her kids especially.

But then it was just a thought. And soon enough, like almost everything else in her life, an afterthought.

Marion plopped down in the white sand, crossed her legs Indian style, covered her face with her hands, and started to weep. Not the howling tears that came along with the flung vase shattering both itself and a photograph on the living room wall after Robert confessed his petty affair; and not the moaning tears from years and years before, the rocking back and forth on the twisted sheets after the miscarriage, back when she thought love could heal anything. No, these tears were silent, drops falling onto her palms, dripping down the inside of her arms to her elbows, falling onto her shorts.

A woman's voice startled her: "Hey there, are you all right? I mean, I'm sorry to intrude, but are you all right?"

Marion lifted her face, the tears and high sun making the blue ocean blurry and blinding, and craned her neck back to where she thought the sound had come from.

"I'm here," the musky voice said again, this time from the other side. "Are you okay?"

A woman, fifties, tanned, blond hair tangled at her shoulders, was squatting two feet away, arms wrapped around her knees.

Marion nodded and closed her eyes, praying that the strange woman would go away when she said nothing.

"Hmmm," the woman said. "Here, take this."

Marion opened her eyes to see what the offering would be: a red scarf with some kind of bird printed on it. She shook her hand and wiped each eye with the back of a hand. "I'm fine," she said. "Thanks," she nodded. "Thanks. I just got some bad news, some hard news, but I'm going to be all right."

"Here," the woman said again, "take this. Your face is a mess of tears and snot. And, you'll have to trust me, there's no chloroform on the cloth to knock you out so I can drag you back into the weeds and take your wallet and jewels. Frankly, you don't look like you have enough cash to make any kind of robbery worthwhile—and, besides," she lifted her upper lip, "in case you're thinking otherwise, I'm not partial to girls."

That made Marion smile. "I haven't been called a girl in decades."

"Take it. It's clean."

Marion took the scarf, opened it up, and wiped it all over her face. When she was done, the long silky material bunched in her fist, she didn't know whether to give it back or stuff it in her shorts. She looked over. "Thanks" was all she could muster.

"No big woop," the woman said. "You sure you're all right?"

"You're not from around here," Marion laughed out loud. "Brooklyn? Long Island?"

"Nope. Chicago. A long time ago. Been all around since then."

Marion blew her nose in the scarf. "I guess I'm going to have to wash this thing out and get it back to you."

"Leslie," the woman said and shrugged. "No matter. There's a lot more where that came from." She paused then, waiting...

"Marion."

"And?"

She smiled again, "Kansas, Wisconsin, North Carolina, and then upstate New York for the first fifty-eight years...and now Manuel Antonio for the last few hours. Nothing to raise an eyebrow at."

Leslie raised an eyebrow.

Two unacquainted men meeting on a beach will circle around each other like wrestlers, sizing each other up, each waiting for the other to suddenly lunge for the take down.

Not so with most women. Within ten minutes, Marion had laid out nearly all the intimate details of her journey from pregnant young grad student who loved animals to devoted wife and mother of three, Den Mother, Girl Scout Leader, "Church Lady"... to "female cuckqueen" (Leslie laughed out loud), eventually becoming the embodiment of Hester Prynne, to a "TV version of Edna Pontellier," abandoned and alone on a beach, about to swim out and drown herself.

Leslie listened patiently to the rest of the tale without a laugh, shook her head when it was done, and said, "I had you all the way up through Hester Prynne—I think I had to read that in ninth grade—but then totally lost you at Edna Pontification or whatever the hell her name was." She patted Marion's small fist, still clutching the red scarf.

———————

"What can I get you lovely senoras?" said the broadly smiling, short, cocoa-skinned man in a white brocaded shirt. The two women were sitting companionably at a small, round, tiled table at Pepe's, a casual open-air café just a few steps from the entrance to Manuel Antonio Park, the small Hotel La Colina just across the dirt road.

"Raymond," Leslie said, "Esta Marion, mi nueva amiga."

Raymond bowed with theatrical graciousness. "Welcome," he said. "What brings you to Manuel Antonio?"

Marion scrunched her lips together, unsure of how much information the question demanded. "Well, I was here a few years ago with my ex-husband...and I've come back now," glancing at Leslie with a thin conspiratorial smile, "without him." Then she shrugged, once again at the edge of tears. She decided it was best not to mention the Habitat for Humanity visit for the time being—to either Raymond or Leslie.

Raymond nodded as if he understood, as if he'd served hundreds of similar women leaving their husbands. "Coffee?"

"Con leche," Leslie said.

"Con leche," Marion parroted her new friend.

When Raymond disappeared into the kitchen, Leslie said, "So ... you've been here before?"

She was nodding before the words moved her tongue: "The first make-up vacation after he cheated on me. Then again maybe a year later with a...church group, but that's a whole other story."

Then there was silence, Raymond coming with the cups of coffee and backing away without a word. "It must have been happy enough if this is the place you've come to—yes?"

"Yes. Maybe. Well, yes, it was beautiful—we stayed at the Karahe Hotel," she pointed back up the road. "I thought we could still work it out, and I loved the Park and the sweet people down here, but I had already—"

Leslie's eyebrows shot up again, and she gestured Marion on with those long fingers, a different colored ring on each one.

Marion responded with a sheepish grin. "I had already slept with his obnoxious best friend," adding as a whispered aside, "...I was vulnerable, I just wanted to hurt him in the worst way, and I felt like such a fraud while the poor man apologized and apologized and pandered to my every whim. He treated me like a queen, and I just couldn't tell him."

"Hmmm...I'm guessing," Leslie grinned, "that's the man you came down here with?"

Marion laughed then, a full-throated laugh. "Oh no no no, that's Jed, our pastor."

Leslie's dark eyes were wide open. "The pastor?"

She nodded, suddenly serious, sorry she had laughed. "Yes, I'm sorry to say. I've just made a mess of everything."

"Marion!" she gasped. "You're my fucking hero!"

Marion beamed in spite of herself. "You must hang around with a strange group of people."

"I do—look at me. But sleeping with the best friend *and* the minister is quite the classic revenge. I mean, we're right back there in the Greek tragedy neighborhood."

Marion shrugged, quietly proud of her sins. "I guess."

Leslie nodded emphatically, then kept twirling and twirling her ringed fingers as Marion told her in some great detail about those months after she answered the phone one afternoon and Robert's client Mara was on the other end.

Marion paused and took a sip of the rich sweet Costa Rican coffee. "I don't know why I'm telling you this. No one—no one in the universe—knows about Garrison. I never told anyone, except the pastor—and you already know how that turned out."

Leslie howled so loud a capuchin monkey lurched out of a tree just above the restaurant.

When it grew quiet, Marion went on, happy to talk to someone who didn't matter, someone who didn't want anything from her. She waited until Leslie looked at her over the raised cup and then went on: "It was just a drunken night…the two of us consoling each other, you know how it goes. I didn't even like him—and I liked him even less afterward. I mean, he cheated on his poor wife, struggling with MS. The more I think about it, the more it just feels like revenge. I wanted to hurt my husband."

Leslie put the empty cup on the tiled table, propped her chin on her hands, and waited for Marion to meet her gaze: "So, is that when you started doing the pastor?"

Marion flinched, then shook her head. "Still a little raw. I don't think I can talk about him right now."

"No problemo." Leslie smiled kindly, reached over the table, and touched her arm. "Anyway, you don't owe me anything."

"Good." Marion said. "Thanks." She glanced around at the darkening jungle. "So distract me—how'd you get here? How do you get by? I mean, what are you doing here?"

"Selling Hecho en Costa Rica scarves."

"Scarves?"

"Yes, scarves, my dear. Like the one you've emptying your tears into. And lots of others." She pulled a big floral handkerchief from her belt, waved it open, and held it wide with both hands at the corners—a green iguana in the middle.

"It's beautiful. I love that lizard!"

"You like this, you should see the monkey, the toucan, the marlin, and the turtle…."

"Do you make these yourself?"

"No." She smiled thinly.

"None of it?"

"No. I don't make or dye or design these things in any way. It's a scam, dear, just like all the 'local pottery' the boys sell on the beach. I buy them in bulk from Indonesia."

"Oh."

"Don't sound so disillusioned, Marion. You're a little too old—and too unchaste—for that. Right?"

Marion frowned, both at the insult and the insight. "You would think. Anyway, I was just thinking about the five pots I bought on the beach that time with Robert."

"The pastor?"

"No, the husband...the ex-husband."

Then there was a silence between the two women.

Marion's eyes grew glassy again.

"Life is hard, Marion. I try not to take it so seriously."

Marion nodded and pointed to the lizard scarf. "Well, if they're all as pretty as that one, I guess it's all good."

"Now you got it."

"So what do you call ...what? The business?"

"Scarves by Leslie."

"Yeah?"

"Yeah." She shifted in her chair, waved the scarf, and said in a smoker's cough voice, "Costa Rican cotton, my own unique designs, and pure native dyes from right here in the Manuel Antonio jungle, mon. They're normally twenty-five dollars, which between you and me is a steal, but you look so be-yoo-tee-ful and so happy, let's make this one fifteen dollars...just for you."

Chapter Thirteen

Not knowing how to get to the Garden District where Jesse Salenger lived, and not wanting to drive the Winnebago around the city, Robert climbed onto a steamy streetcar heading down Esplanade to the Quarter. When they got to Canal, the driver told him he had to change cars, which he did, dropping himself down hard on the wooden bench, his shirt sticking to his back, sweat dripping onto his lap as they rounded Lee Circle and clanged up St. Charles Avenue to Second Street. This was taking much, much longer than he anticipated.

Jesse had told him that his house was on the corner of Second and Coliseum, number 1402. "This is no fucking house," Robert muttered, standing at the six-foot wrought-iron fence and looking up at the enormous cream-colored Italianate mansion. He turned the brass knob and pushed against the heavy gate, walking along the wide bluestone path to the even wider and more gracious steps. When he looked up, Jesse was standing behind the tall glass door, dwarfed by the massive windows on either side, the same 23-year-old smirk on his old friend's 60-year-old face.

They embraced like old pals, but right from the start it didn't feel right. It had been such a long time since he and Jesse were friends, decades really. Even then, they were more roommates than friends and, later, nothing more than occasional drinking buddies

Jesse placed his hand on his old buddy's shoulder and led him into a massive living room, 16-foot ceiling at least, a fireplace in the middle and another at the end, formal furniture groupings in three separate areas, and three of the biggest nearly threadbare Oriental rugs Robert had ever seen defining each one.

Robert turned up his palms and laughed, "Holy crap, Jesse, what did you do? Rob a fucking bank? Discover a cure for..." he couldn't think of anything, "...what? Aging? Unhappiness?"

The smirk on Jesse's face, the same one he wore when they first saw each other on either side of the glass, grew into a yellow-toothed smile. "A little of this, a little of that, my old friend. Hard to explain, really, it's a different world down here than in Chapel Hill—or in New York City." He said "New York City" like Burl Ives playing Big Daddy would have said it.

Robert was stung. In that unremarkable instant, he remembered how silently contentious it once was between the two of them—especially with the unspoken specter of Marion between them, despite Jesse's disclaimers at the time. His response was lame: "Never lived in Manhattan, Jesse. I...well, Marion and I lived upstate in a little college town, Elting...you knew that."

Salenger shrugged as if he was in session with a client. "All the same to me, old man. A Yankee is a Yankee is a Yankee." He laughed, a smoker's laugh. "Tell me what you're doing down here."

Just then Robert's cell rang: no nonsense tones for him, rather, tones he had chosen as a silent protest to all the silly songs and chirping birds it seemed everyone else in Elting programmed theirs to play. The ringing was so startling—it was the first call, the only call, he had received since he left home—that he fumbled through several pockets until he located the phone.

Sam Tevis was written across the small screen.

"Sam!" he called out, gleeful.

Sam was more subdued. "Hey, Pop, where are you?"

"Down in the Delta," he crooned, instantly sorry that he was putting on airs and quickly correcting himself. "New Orleans. I arrived a couple of days ago. I'm here with an old friend from grad school."

"That's nice, that's nice," Sam said and paused.

Robert's smile faded."What's wrong, Sam?" He gestured to Jesse and walked back into the large foyer.

"Oh…it's really not so wrong as much as I, um, don't know what to do. Mom called." He took a breath.

"From Costa Rica? Is she sick?"

"No no no…she's fine. It's just that she and Jed split up and…I don't know what to tell her."

Tell her to go fuck herself, Robert thought, but said instead, "Well, what does she need you to do? Is she stuck there? I mean, does she need you to take care of anything?"

"She didn't ask for anything. She just called and told me that they'd separated and I figured, well, I don't know what I figured. She sounded kind of teary. That's pretty much what I'm calling about. She's all alone. Do you think I should go down?"

"No, son, I don't think that's wise," Robert said, that psychoanalytic tone weaseling its way back into his larynx. "She's a big girl. You know your mother, she's pretty resilient. Anyway, if she wanted you to come down there and help her pick up the pieces, I'm pretty sure…I'm sure she would have asked."

"But—"

"But—" Robert cut him off and then cut himself off. "I take that back. There's a lot about your mom I really don't know. If you want to go, you should go, Sam."

"Alyssa thinks it was a cry for help."

Robert laughed. "And when did Alyssa get her PhD in counseling? I know your mother as well as anyone in the world, Sam, and I truly suspect it was just a cry."

"Okay. But should I call her again?" Sam sounded deflated.

"You know, you don't have to parent us, Sam."

"But—"

"But yes, absolutely, call her." He walked back into the massive living room. "And tell her that I'm visiting Jesse Salenger in New Orleans. That'll perk her up. And when you get a chance, call me back sometime and let me know how you're doing." Then he added, "And everyone else."

Thus chastised, Sam tried to explain how busy he'd been before the pause that initiated the two of them offering up their awkward good-byes ("Kiss Glenda and Aaron for me"), leaving Robert to wonder what kept him from just giving his son the approval he always so desperately sought.

Then he turned off the ringer.

The afternoon was excruciating, Jesse bloviating about the Garden District and his board memberships and his children, both lawyers, and his wife, the director of gifts at Trinity, and eventually, two bourbons in, how lucky the two of them were to escape Marion. "Too bad it took you so goddamn long to save your soul," he said with a hoarse laugh, reaching into the humidor to pick out two Cubans.

Robert shrugged at the inference and declined the offer of the cigar. And two hours later, when Jesse extended an ahem-laden invitation to dinner and then accepted Robert's regrets before the complete litany of excuses were out of his mouth, he couldn't wait to get out of there.

Jesse put up a hand, "Another time, old buddy. We're not so slow down here that we don't understand pootang!" Then he smiled, rising from a wing chair. "Promise me you'll come back sometime and meet my Minerva." He winked then, as if Robert should connect the dots. "Besides, I want to know how this great adventure of yours turns out. I can't wait to tell Minerva about that Mountain person and the others."

Robert set the glass of watery bourbon on a coaster and, with an unintended groan as he pressed his palms into his knees, unstuffed himself from the overstuffed couch.

At the massive front door, Jesse looked like he was just about to offer his arms in a salutary hug, but Robert stiffened his resolve not to lie and extended his swollen hand. Jesse took it in both of his, "Damn good to see you, old friend. We had some good times back in Chapel Thrill."

Robert smiled, graciously he hoped, and walked down the steps and across the wide bluestone path to the gate, already reaching into his breast pocket for Jen Magruder's card with one hand and digging deep into his pants pocket with the other for his cell phone.

He found a missed call from Marion.

There was no message, just a missed call. Tempted to leave it at that, adopting the shrink voice for himself—*If she had wanted you to call back, she would have left a message*—but he simply couldn't leave it at just that. Especially after Sam's call. Especially since he knew what he knew. Especially because he was aimless—and virtually friendless in the world.

So he pushed the call button and seconds later heard, "Oh Robert, thank you for calling me back! I didn't leave a message because I didn't think you would call me back."

"What is it, Marion?" he asked, now beyond the heavy wrought iron gate and walking slowly up towards the trolleys on St. Charles Avenue. "Is something wrong?"

"No…yes…well, more of a glitch than anything."

"Yes, Sam called—"

"Sam called?"

He stopped walking then, standing on the corner of Prytania, momentarily concerned that he'd betrayed his son. "Oh, you know Sam, he can't help himself," he said, not really sure what he meant.

Marion laughed. "I do indeed…but what, pray tell, did our very good son tell you?"

"It was just that you and Jed had separated…and he wanted to know if he should do anything."

"What did you tell him?"

"He wanted to know if he should go down there."

Her voice was deeper now. "Well, as soon as you get off, you call him back and tell him to stay put. Oh Lord, that's just about the last thing I need right now."

There was a pause. He was thinking *I don't take orders from you anymore, Marion. Call him yourself.* But what he said was "I think it best you call him yourself." His heart was pounding like he was a teenager talking back to a teacher—or his own mother.

Then it was her turn to grow silent. "I'm sorry, Robert, I didn't mean—I'm just so at loose ends down here…."

Robert waited for her to continue and when she didn't, he said as coolly as possible, "Well, what can I do for you, Marion?"

"Oh Robert, it's just an oversight from when we were divvying up the property."

"Yeah?" He crossed Prytania.

"Well," she said, "it's the vacation account that we set up a long time ago, and we agreed—"

"I know," he cut her off, "what it is, Marion—and I remember what we agreed upon. What do you want?"

"Well, it seems that we never changed the names on the account…and since it's a joint account, I—"

A green streetcar was approaching; Robert ran across to the other side of the median. "So, what do you want me to do, Marion?"

"I need you to sign an affidavit that attests to—"

"Marion," he started, reaching into his pocket and finding five quarters, "you know that I'm not home, I don't have an address, a lawyer, anything. I mean, really, I'm just this side of homeless. I'm living in a fucking RV." He climbed up the three steps into the streetcar, let the quarters slip from his swollen hand, and lumbered to the back.

"But Robert, I really need that money right now—it's too complicated to explain—and it is my money, you know. I just need—"

He sat down on an empty bench just as the streetcar lurched forward, headed uptown toward Fourth Street. "Marion, I'm more than a thousand miles away from Elting, so I don't know how in the hell I could possibly help you."

She was weepy now, her voice thick. "I'm sorry. I'm really sorry. But I'm really at loose ends, Robert…couldn't you please, just this once—" She stopped then.

Looking out toward a park and wondering if it was the Audubon Park he read about in the *Lonely Planet* guide, Robert resisted another unseemly urge, which was to tell her to fuck off, and said in his old, married, annoyed voice, "I'm busy right now, Marion, I have a date." He paused, letting it sink in. "But I'll see what I can do tomorrow."

"Thank you very much, Robert. That would mean a lot to me."

"Call me tomorrow," he said, closing the phone before she finished saying good-bye. He imagined her at the other end muttering something like *"Fuck you Dr. Pompous Ass Psychotherapist! You can go shove the goddamn bank account up your hairy ass for all I care."*

Ten minutes later, the streetcar having moved up the oak-shaded St. Charles Avenue, gracious mansions on either side, was up near the turn at Carrollton. It stopped, Cooter Brown's Tavern & Oyster Bar on the left, the Camellia Grill on the right, and a large woman sidled in next to him. Despite his displeasure at having to share the bench, Robert was unexpectedly quite happy with himself, having remembered Carrollton from earlier in the day and figuring—as it turned out, quite incorrectly— that the streetcar would take him back to where he had parked the Winnebago and gone off with Jen Magruder.

And with that, he pulled the card out of his breast pocket again and punched in her number.

"Yeah?" she answered.

"Jen Magruder, please," he said, not sure how to just say hello.

"Yeah?"

"Hi …hi, Jen, this is Robert. Robert Tevis from earlier this afternoon?"

"Hey there, Bobby, what's shakin'?"

"Um, nothing much, just on the streetcar, heading back to the RV and wondering if you still want to meet for dinner?" His throat was dry.

"Dinner?"

"Yeah," he said, shifting away from the woman next to him. "We talked about going to Mother's I think?"

"Right, right, right…Mother's. I was just writing up another review and closed my eyes for a few—and you know how it is, I got myself a little confused. Are you paying? I don't pay for food anymore."

"I am," he smiled.

"Sounds like an offer I can't refuse. Are you gonna pick me up like a proper date, Bobby?"

"Well, if you're not too ashamed to drive around in a Winnebago, I'll pick you up."

"I'm staying at a friend's place—912 Picheloup Place. You know where that is? Of course you don't know where that is. Well, from City Park, go down Carrollton to Dumaine, make a left, and Picheloup is two blocks up. 9-1-2."

"I'll be there in I'm guessing twenty minutes," he said.

Twenty minutes later, Robert was standing at the end of the line on Carrollton, looking around. Nothing was familiar. He waited while a group of black kids sauntered by, laughing and pushing each other off the median, and then stopped an older woman.

She said she'd never heard of Picheloup Place in all her years in the city. "What about Audubon Park?"

She told him to get back on the streetcar and look for the park on his right. Twenty-five minutes later—now twenty-five minutes late—he got off at Audubon Park, turned around and around, finally asking a college girl where Dumaine might be.

She shrugged and said she'd never heard of it.

When he called Jen to apologize, she burst into laughter. "First, you're on the wrong streetcar line—and second, I told you City Park, not Audubon Park—and third, why the hell didn't you ask me?"

He shrugged, insulted of course, but kept that to himself as well. "I'm wondering about that myself these days."

"Well, Bobby, take it from me, you are a doof—hard to believe you got a PhD—or maybe that doctorate explains everything."

"Yeah," he conceded, the stirring in his loins somehow overriding the hurt pride. "I am lost. What do I do, Jen?"

She told him to stay right where he was. Told him, like she was talking to a lost fifth grader, that he should sit himself down in the gazebo on the Exposition Boulevard side of the park. "I'll be by in, like, half an hour. I'm driving a beat-to-shit Jeep Wrangler ragtop, red—I'll honk. Don't wander off, and for Christ's sake don't get back on the streetcar."

A bowl of gumbo, an Abita, a Styrofoam dish of steaming

crawfish etouffe, some collards, a helping of bread pudding, another Abita, and Jen Magruder's hand every so often rubbing the inside of his knee made the glorious food the most sensuous meal of his life. The bill paid, Robert could not wait to get back into the red Jeep and cruise, top down, through the humid night air and into the long smooth arms of a smooth-skinned lover who didn't want to be healed, who didn't want him to sign anything, who wanted nothing more than the only love a man like him could offer.

When they pulled up in front of 912 Picheloup, she reached over and patted his thigh, those long, thin, ringed fingers lingering between knee and heaven, "So…cuppa?"

"Coffee?" he asked, grinning.

"Coffee," she answered cooly. "Don't you start thinking that I'm gonna sleep with you, Bobby, just cause you bought me dinner. And don't start thinking this is anything more than you and me sharing some quality time along the way. I got other things on my mind."

He was about to deny that sex was the only thing on his mind, but something hard to explain had happened that afternoon with Jesse and with Marion, and now he didn't have the will to play the game anymore. "Does that mean you're not going to sleep with me? Or you're going to sleep with me, but not because I bought you dinner?"

Jen raised her eyebrows and lifted her hand as if to tell him to stop right where he was.

"I was kind of hoping," he continued through her warning silence, "that it was the latter, you know, that you're going to sleep with me, but not because I sprung for dinner."

"Oh, I gotcha, Bobby." She cut him off, patting his thigh again. "But I'm afraid there's no brass ring for you tonight. I don't sleep with men I just met. Bad practice, that. And keep in mind, big guy, we're just around to help each other get to the next place we need to go. All of us."

Robert got out of the Jeep, politely thanked her for a nice evening, walked away down Picheloup, and made a left on Dumaine.

"Wrong direction!" she called out.

He looked back, surprised to see her still on the porch. He waved his hand, "Right."

Then he turned around and, striding toward Carrollton, Robert felt how alone—and lonely—he was in the world. And by the time he returned to the Winnebago, he understood for the first time that night that he really needed to help Marion get her money.

Chapter Fourteen

Continental Air flight 1707 arrived in San Jose, Costa Rica, at 12:54 p.m. At Sam Tevis's urging, he, his wife Glenda, and their eight-year-old son Aaron, remained in their row of three seats, waiting until the aisle had cleared.

"I just don't know why people are so anxious to stand in line," he said, just as he did every time they flew somewhere.

Glenda, blonde and pixie-ish was sitting next to Sam, whose Eastern European roots and size made him look like a bear. She patted him on the thigh, "It's a real conundrum, Sammy."

Aaron slid off the seat and stood next to the window, crumbs from his box of Goldfish falling onto his shoes and the carpet. "Let's go!" he said, adding a flat, upstate New York "Arrib-er! Arrib-er!" which he had just learned in his third grade Spanish class.

Glenda laughed.

Sam was still on edge. "We'll just wait until the row clears, A-man."

Aaron plopped back on the seat and took out his Game Boy.

Glenda took Sam's hand and whispered, "It will be all right, big man. You can stop being a vice-principal for a few days."

After an hour and a half of customs lines, stop-and-go revolving luggage belts, and a short ride in a clunky airport transport to the Alamo car rental, the Tevis family was almost on the road. But not before Juan Marichel, the sweating Alamo manager, gave Sam the car keys and the warning he gives all renters: "Senor, don't forget to lock the car every time you get out. Don't leave anything of value in the car. And when you're on the beach," he looked down at the contract, "in Manuel Antonio, don't leave your wallet or purse or anything else of value unattended. "

"Why?" Aaron asked as soon as they were driving off, the air conditioner blowing warm, then cool air on their sweaty faces, Sam behind the wheel of the little Corolla and Glenda reading the map that Senor Marichel had given them, with a thick line, added in red marker, running west over the mountains from San Jose and south to Manuel Antonio.

"Why what?" asked Sam.

"Why do you have watch your stuff on the beach?"

Sam looked in the rearview mirror at his skinny blond boy strapped into the seat belt. "Because people might steal it."

"Why?"

Sam didn't know what to say, so he said, "Well, for one, because there are a lot of poor people in Costa Rica and—"

Glenda then did what she often did as a high school English teacher: stopped him before he got himself into trouble. "Because people might steal our stuff, that's all, Aaron."

Aaron looked blank, like he'd already forgotten what he had asked. "When are we going to get there?"

"Settle in, buddy," Sam said, following Glenda's finger and making a left onto CN27 toward Orotino. "The man at the car rental place said it will take us three hours."

It turned out that "three hours" was three hours of languid Costa Rican time. After navigating the windy, narrow roads on Carreterra Nacionale 34 through Tarcoles, Herradura, Jaco, Parrita, and a late lunch in the most beautiful hillside café Sam had ever seen overlooking the lushest valley Sam had ever seen, they were still an hour or two outside of Quepos.

And Qupeos was where Marion was waiting for them, three

hours late at 5:30. She was jumping up and down and waving like a crazy woman on the sidewalk in front of the Auto Mercado. Right next to her was a woman wearing a flowing scarf of some kind, smiling perhaps a little too serenely.

Chapter Fifteen

Aaron was the first out of the car, leaping into Marion's outstretched arms and instantly laying his head on her shoulder and going limp. For a moment she feared that he was crying, but soon realized that for the little boy, it was just pure relief to be back in his grandmother's soft arms, on her soft bosom, once again.

Glenda hopped out next. She stretched a yoga stretch and leaned back on the car until Aaron let go, slipping slowly slowly slowly out of Marion's arms down to the sidewalk.

"You look wonderful, Marion," Glenda cooed.

"I'm miserable," Marion whispered in her ear and then stepped back, her hands still on Glenda's shoulders, the warm smile still on her face. "And you look great…beautiful!"

Glenda smiled. "Well, if hot, tired, sweaty, nauseous, and annoyed lead to beauty, I must be in line for Miss America."

Then Sam was suddenly there, one big hairy arm around each of their backs, pulling them into his embrace. "So good to have both my girls back in my arms." His eyes were pooling.

Marion was the first to break the silence, looking her daughter-in-law in the eye. "Does he sometimes want to make you stick your finger all the way down your throat?"

Glenda laughed out loud. "Only occasionally," she said.

Sam dropped his arms to his sides like a little boy.

"Oh Sammy…I don't I don't I don't," Glenda giggled. "I just said that because your mom was being…that was mean, Marion!"

Marion turned to her son and reached up to place her hands on both sides of his full face, "Oh Sam, I was just teasing you."

She was going to let it go at that, but his trip down there had irked her and suddenly she couldn't stop herself. "But Sam, sweetheart, please don't ever call me a 'girl.' I'm fifty-eight-years-old, a mother, an underachiever, an adulterer, a grandmother. I'm fat and I'm all alone in this jungle, and I am, what? I mean, what am I?"

"Gloriously happy to see your grandchild!" Leslie chirped up from behind.

Glenda tilted her head, wondering who the strange woman might be, looking her up and down as if admiring her barefoot elegant style. Sam glowered, clearly thinking something sinister was going on.

This inspired Marion to offer brief introductions, presenting Leslie as "my best friend in all of Costa Rica." Aaron, as if on cue, grabbed his grandmother around the waist, almost toppling both of them, and everyone laughed the loud laugh of the dispossessed.

Marion asked Sam if Aaron could ride with her, pointing to the blue Corolla, whereupon the boy raced over and jumped in his Gram's car without his father's approval, just a warning to buckle his seat belt. Fifteen minutes later, the two-car caravan was parking on the hillside way above the white sand beach at Manuel Antonio.

Aaron ran right into the cottage, scampering around the mostly empty rooms, racing out onto the vast veranda overlooking the lush valley, shrieking at the monkeys swinging through the trees, screaming at the iguanas who, unused to such exuberance, scurried down below and disappeared under the deck. It was just what Marion needed to raise her spirits.

While Sam went back out to lug in the bags, Marion showed Glenda the breezy guest room, a ceiling fan whirring from the exposed rafters. "Oh Marion, this is—" she started to say, but then just spread her arms and twirled around and around until Sam came in sweating profusely and dropped the suitcases with a thud on the wooden floor.

Glenda glanced over at Marion. "I think we need to get out of these hot city clothes."

And a few minutes later Glenda walked out of the bedroom wearing melon-colored shorts and a white tank top—too white, Marion thought, for her too-pale New York skin. "This is heaven, Marion,"

"Well, it was supposed to be heaven," Marion said. She walked out on the veranda, where Aaron was still shrieking at the monkeys, and held the boy close from behind. She remembered holding his father in the same way on the porch at Mohonk. "I don't know," she called back into the cottage, now looking out into the descending jungle, "maybe it still can be."

"What are you going to do, Mom?" she heard from the kitchen, where Sam was making gin and tonics for the three of them.

"What am I going to do about what?" she called over her shoulder, still holding on to Aaron.

"This place. What are you going to do with it?"

"I'm going to live in it, what do you think?"

Glenda was at the sliding doors then, holding a pink concoction with a lime that Leslie had made for Aaron. Sam was behind. "I just figured you would sell it and come back to Elting," he said, extending the first glass to Glenda and then the other to Marion.

"Why would I go back to Elting?"

Glenda raised her glass: "First, let's toast this beautiful house in this beautiful country and the beautiful woman who lured us down here."

Marion felt herself getting weepy again, but as she'd been weepy for nearly a month already, she was getting better at climbing up and over it. "You are a sweetheart, Glenda—thank you. And thank you, Sammy," she raised her glass, "for coming down to see me," she lowered her eyelids, "and for forgiving me my awful trespasses."

Sam shook his head. "There are no trespasses in—" he started to say, but clearly didn't know what to say next.

Marion was too impatient to wait for Sam's awkward declaration. "I do want to clear up something, Sam: I'm not going back to Elting, not now, not later. Not ever. I did a terrible thing, yes, but my friends treated me in a hateful way, and for that alone, I'm never going back there. For better and worse, this is where I'm putting down my roots."

"But we're all back there," Sam said so plainly and so plaintively.

"Well, not all of you, Sam—you do have a sister in Asheville and a father...somewhere. Last I spoke to him he was in New Orleans. And while I guess there are easier places to find oneself, this one is pretty damn good. And look around. It's pretty easy to settle into."

"But you belong back with us, Mom. You're all alone here."

"I am not. I have my good friend, Leslie..." Marion made a sweeping gesture with her arm that she expected would elicit a bow from Leslie, but her new friend was nowhere to be seen. "Well, I guess Leslie decided to leave us alone with all of our nuclear family tensions. But you'll see her again tomorrow for dinner."

"So it's just you and this Leslie character?"

Marion smiled, "Yeah, a real character. And a few new friends who are writers, it turns out. And, for worse rather than better, Jed is still here." She looked at Glenda, "Hair shirt and all."

Glenda laughed.

Sam frowned. "I'm sorry to have to say this, Mom, but you're not getting any younger. You shouldn't be alone at your age— and so far away from family. I thought—"

"Is that why you came? To lure me back to Elting?"

"No no no, Marion." Glenda slid in like one of the spider monkeys swinging through the trees. "We came to see you. Really. Aaron asks for you every single day. And, of course, we always wanted to see Costa Rica, especially after all those amazing, gorgeous pictures you and, you know, brought back when you were down here."

"Robert," Marion said. "You can say his name."

Sam was obviously tagged as the second chorus: "Aaron has been begging to see you all winter."

"He has," Glenda concurred. "And let's be honest," she grinned, "it's been freakin' cold in Elting for months."

Marion gave her the scowl she usually reserved for Sam. "Well, that's a real inducement to go back to a place where my name might as well be Hester Prynne."

"Who?" Sam said.

"Oh my." She smiled and walked over to give her overgrown boy a sweet kiss on the cheek. "I am such a failure."

When a cell phone rang a few moments later, Sam leaped off the couch and loped into the bedroom, passing Glenda who strode past him into the living room, tossing sweaters and jackets off the couch in search of her purse. Marion hovered in the doorway. She had no idea where her phone was.

Sam walked out of the bedroom, "Not mine."

"Not mine either," said Glenda, her hand still fiddling around inside the big bag, adding, "must be…" when the ringing started again, now clearly coming from beneath the couch. Aaron dove under and emerged with a beat-up flip phone.

"Oh," Marion laughed, "that's mine! I've been looking for the damn thing all day."

She took the phone from Aaron and, expecting it to be Leslie, opened it without checking the screen. "Hola!" she said brightly.

"Mom…"

"Alyssa!" She turned, whispering to Sam, "It's Alyssa!" She was happy for that one instant to have her two oldest babies in reach. But when her daughter didn't start talking immediately, she grew worried. "Is something the matter, darling?"

"Well…I'm sorry to break in down there, I know that Sam and everyone must've just got there, but—"

"But what?"

"I just got a call from a hospital in Mexico City. They said that Dad was in the hospital. He had a stroke."

After an hour, and six increasingly hysterical calls later to the Centro Medico ABC (the American British Cowdray Medical Center) in Mexico City, Marion had left Sam sitting on the veranda and gone off to find Leslie (who was not answering her cell). In the midst of all the bilingual wrangling and yelling that went on between Sam and various hospital administrators, Glenda had taken Aaron to the beach. Marion hoped to find Leslie at her studio, with the expectation that Leslie would be better able to talk to—and understand—the Mexican doctors.

Driving over to Leslie's place, imagining Robert paralyzed on one side, lying in a hospital bed with tubes and wires connecting him to unearthly machines, it was as if the last several years of agonizing hurt and betrayal had faded away into the frightful present.

Pulling up in front of what Leslie called her *caseta*, Marion was still babbling to herself, imagining Leslie's objections, explaining that while she didn't love him anymore, he was still her family, he was her children's father, she couldn't erase the thirty-five years they were together, she'd known him longer than anyone in the world.

Leslie wasn't home, so Marion ran down to the beach. She wasn't there either. Or at the café.

The sun was a massive orange ball of fire over the Pacific and the jungle was quiet and still for the first time that day when Marion finally returned home, breathless and sweaty. "I couldn't find her," she said.

"It's all right, Mother," Sam said, patting the cushion beside him. "Sit down. I never got to speak directly to Dad, but he's okay."

Her eyes were red from crying. "Who did you speak with?" she demanded.

"A friend of Dad's." He looked a bit sheepish. "She was the one who finally answered his cell phone."

"Who?"

"I don't know, a woman named Jennifer. She was very nice and—"

Marion looked confused. "I don't know a Jennifer."

"I don't either. She must be a friend of his, I don't know. I haven't spoken to him in a month or more."

"I spoke to him two weeks ago. He didn't say where he was."

"Listen, Mom: The woman, Jennifer, said he was fine, he was resting, and she'd make sure he calls us tomorrow. She said he had what might have been a stroke, but he's fine now."

"How could he have a stroke and be fine?"

"I don't know."

She watched from the veranda as he made his way into the kitchen, pouring some gin into a dirty glass and, grabbing some flat warm tonic from the counter, filling it to the top.

Marion called, "Isn't there some doctor there who can tell us what's happening?"

He gritted his teeth. "No." He took a big gulp of his drink. "I just talked to Alyssa. She's going to fly down there tomorrow to make sure they're treating him okay."

She was shaking her head. "Someone's got to call Beryl."

"I'll call her. Later. After we get a chance to speak to Dad directly. I've gotta get down to the beach now and find Aaron and Glenda—she's probably worried sick."

"No. I should call Beryl."

Now Sam was shaking his head. "There's no sense in worrying her until we know what's happening. You know how she is." He finished off the warm gin and tonic. "Besides, that Jennifer person said he was fine, so let's just wait until Dad calls us tomorrow. She promised he would."

But Marion had already dialed Beryl, turning and walking back into the cottage when the phone started to ring.

"Mom?"

"Hi, sweet pea, I um—"

"I'm kind of in a rush, Mom, late for class—so I gotta make it quick. What's up in paradise?"

Marion realized she had no idea how to respond.

"Mom! Are you all right?"

"I'm fine, darling, but your dad is in the hospital...."

Chapter Sixteen

Alyssa Rodgers strode into the massive lobby of the ABC Medical Center in Mexico City and immediately stopped to look all around—at the four-story-high ceiling, the vast reproduction of a Diego Rivera mural on one wall, the streaming indoor waterfall on another. Shiny, curved desks. A glass-enclosed gift shop off to the side. Crisp security guards. Not at all what she had imagined.

"May I assist you, Senora?" asked a young man in a khaki uniform, a carbine slung across his chest. His voice was soft and kind.

"I'm looking for my father...mi padre," she said, reaching all the way back to Spanish III at Hardwick. "Está...enferma?"

He bowed his head and grasped her elbow, leading her over to the large curved desk in the center of the lobby.

The receptionist spoke English, as did the elevator operator, as did the floor nurse up on the eighth floor. So it turned out that after the cab ride, Alyssa didn't have to use the *Fodor's* phrase book she had bought at JFK. She was trembling as she rode the elevator up to the eighth floor, out of breath walking down the quiet hall, and tearing up by the time she reached the closed door to Room 814. But it wasn't until she saw her father asleep in bed #2, a canula in his nose, an IV in his bruised arm, that she burst into tears, all the anger about the divorce and leaving Elting dissolving in the antiseptic air.

He was alone, no roommate for now. Alysssa stood over him, tears flowing over her high cheekbones and falling onto her breasts. He did not stir, as she'd assumed he would as soon as he sensed her presence. So she wiped her eyes with the back of her hand and reached over the chrome bed rail, touching his warm wrist, waiting until his eyes fluttered open.

"Lyssa?" He smiled up at her. "Am I dreaming?"

"No." She smiled back at him, a smile that quickly gave way to sobs. "Oh, Daddy...are you...?"

She was squeezing his wrist so tightly that he winced. "Sorry," she said.

"I'm fine, sweetheart. In fact, I should be out of here in a day or two." He raised the other arm, the one with the IV. "They're supposed to be taking this damn contraption out of me this morning." He looked over at the closed door. "No one told me you were coming...."

Alyssa pulled the yellow naugahyde-covered chair over to her father's bedside and told him how she'd left the kids with her husband and gotten the first plane out of JFK as soon as she'd heard the news.

He reached for her hand and told her all about the "incident," what he called a "transient ischemic attack," at a restaurant outside Mexico City. "...pins and needles up and down my arm," lifting the IV-ed hand again, "and, the really scary thing, for maybe an hour or two, I couldn't speak...I could think what I wanted to say, but I couldn't get it to my tongue."

Alyssa closed her eyes, tears slipping out the corners and down her wet cheeks. "I'm so..."

Robert let go of her hand and reached up to brush the tears away. "It was pretty awful," he said grimly.

She took his wrist again, softer this time. "But how...how did you get here...this place is—"

"Yeah, quite amazing," he finished her sentence. "Nothing like I imagined while I was flat on my back and strapped to a gurney, two guys named Hector driving me through the barrio."

Alyssa looked back at the closed door and lowered her voice. "I didn't know what to expect…I don't know, chickens in the lobby, some scene out of Cheech and Chong, a marimba band…," now flashing that smirky smile he knew so well from years past.

"Well, turns out I was really lucky to be with someone who knew what to do. She called for an ambulance and told them to take me to ABC. They apparently wanted to go someplace else a little closer, but she insisted—"

"Who?"

He inadvertently lifted the arm with the IV and winced. "Just a friend I made in New Orleans."

Her voice turned cooler, prosecutorial. "Do I know her?"

Robert laughed, his mouth slightly askew. "A friend of mine, Commandante."

"Sorry." She lowered her eyes. "But who was this angel of mercy?" She was smiling again.

"Her name is Jennifer Magruder, she's a freelance food writer—and she's been traveling with me since New Orleans."

"It was San Antone, Bobby," came a bright voice from the suddenly open doorway. Alyssa spun around and locked eyes with another long-haired woman. "I 'spect this must be one of your progeny," the woman said, holding out her browned hand. "Jen Magruder."

"Alyssa." She didn't take the woman's hand, the coolness returning to her voice. "Alyssa Rodgers, Dr. Tevis's daughter."

Jen stood there with her hand extended. "Don't just leave me hangin' here, girl."

"Oh sorry," Alyssa said, taking her hand from her father's wrist and shaking hands with his—friend? Girlfriend? Whore? "Well, my dad was just telling me that you basically saved his life."

"I doubt it, given that he was almost all better by the time we arrived in this joint. But it's nice that he thinks so."

"Either way, I want to thank you. We were all really worried about him back home."

There was a brief uncomfortable silence when she slipped her hand from Jen's, and then Jen was jabbering on about some "out-of-this-world chalupa joint" she just came from in "Colonia Centro…which is arguably the seediest neighborhood in all of Ciudad de Mexico."

Alyssa frowned at the Spanish. She tilted her head and the prosecutorial voice returned: "So are you two, um—"

"Sleeping together?" Jen said brightly and glanced over at Robert with a wicked grin.

He coughed. "Hey!"

Alyssa swallowed her repulsion. "Well, I wasn't actually asking that. Having never heard your name before, I was just curious to know what your relationship is."

Jen turned to the bed. Robert seemed to be enjoying the jousting match that was just beginning: "So, just how would you define our relationship, Herr Doctor Tevis?"

He tilted his head and offered a wry smile. "I don't know, maybe friends with benefits?"

"Oh, Jesus Christ, Dad!" Alyssa now looked down into her lap. "This is totally gross. I mean, how do you even know that term?"

He laughed out loud, reaching through the rail for her hand. "I'm just teasing you, Alyssa. We're friends, mostly. We definitely do a lot of eating together, which is probably why I'm here in this hospital bed."

Alyssa glared at Jen. "He's a sick man, you know. He's got CHF and, and I don't know if he told you how old he is—"

"Oh, I know a lot about him, darlin'—including sucking down all those ACE inhibitors and such—but don't you worry, I have no designs on being your new mommy."

Alyssa didn't laugh.

"In fact, now that you're here to take care of the old goat, I'm gonna be movin' on. I'm already a few days behind schedule and there's a cantina in Taxco that I'm supposed to review like yesterday."

Robert's countenance shifted like a cloud passing over the sun. "Just like that?"

Jennifer walked around and scrunched in on the other side of the bed. "Yeah," her voice softer now, "I was gonna talk to you tomorrow." She reached over for his shoulder and slid her hand into the loose hospital gown sleeve. "I was gonna stick around until you got out of the hospital and had it all figured out where you're going next. But now that your daughter is here, I really am behind schedule for *Lonely Planet*—and the God's honest truth is that you can't be traveling with me anymore, Bobby. Lord, I just about killed you with the chalupas and the po'boys and the late hours and," raising her eyebrows, "everything else."

Alyssa flinched noticably at the "everything else." Then looked disgusted.

Robert was silent for what seemed like a long time. "What am I going to do?" he finally said, not directing it to either woman.

Alyssa started to say something, but Jen cut in, "That's probably something you want to be discussing with your daughter, Bobby. I'm gonna haul my sorry ass over to the Winnebago, pack up my stuff, make a few calls, and cut the Wrangler loose."

Alyssa had never seen her father so close to tears, not even when her mother left him.

Jennifer stroked his shoulder. "I'll be back later, early evening, to say good-bye, Bobby." She stood then and leaned over and gave him a kiss on his unshaven cheek. "Nice to meet you, Alyssa— maybe I'll catch you later." She held out her hand across the bed, and Alyssa took it with a single shake.

"Thank you again," she said.

"Glad I was around."

Alyssa nodded and watched Jen walk around the foot of the bed and out of the room. When Jen was out of sight, her footsteps receding into the beeping that seemed to be all around, Alyssa held out her hand and sneered, "Don't leave me hangin'!"

And when her father didn't say anything, she added, "That is one ill-mannered, uneducated woman, Dad. I mean, in what back alley did you find that skank?"

That made him smile. "Well, my dear daughter, it's somehow comforting that you're as edgy as ever."

"And what's up with her calling you Bobby?"

"Wasn't that kind of sweet?"

"No! What's happened to you? Actually, it's rude and disrespectful. You're a man of some substance. What the hell is she?"

Robert lifted his stubbly chin and tilted his head to the side, "I'd say she's kind of sweet."

She pressed her lips together, then smoothed the wild hair on his head. "Well, I think you're losing it, old man. But now that I'm here, we're going to get you back on the right track. And the first thing we're gonna do once you get out of this joint is get you a haircut." She ran her fingers like a rake through his longer-than-it-had-ever-been hair and growled, "Ugh, greasy!"

"Don't be so certain of getting me back on any track, sweet Alyssa. I am a changed man—and I'm never going back."

She nodded. "Right. You keep believing that, old man. But mark my words, you are headed straight back to Elting as soon as I get everything figured out down here."

He squared his chin. "Over my dead body, darling. Mark my words."

"Oh, Dad!" She softened then. Kissed his hand, held it to her cheek. "Please don't."

He laughed. "I'm not going to die."

"Good!" she said with a smile, wanting to sound cheerful for her father's sake. "Well, right now I've got some calls to make. I already have five missed calls from Sam. Do you want to speak to him?"

He shook his head, readjusted the nasal canula. "He's going to cry and make me feel sicker than I already am."

"Okay."

"And in case you're thinking otherwise, I don't want to speak to your mother either."

But within minutes, Alyssa was listening to her father's side of a heated conversation with her mother.

"Marion, with all due respect, I don't want to be discussing any of this with you. I already told your daughter that I didn't want to talk with you, but she apparently thinks that I am a doddering old fool who has lost his mind and thus doesn't need to be listened to. I mean, Jesus fucking Christ, Marion, I am only sixty years old and—"

Alyssa could hear her mother's dry, tinny reply coming through the receiver. "And you've had a stroke."

"Good-bye, Marion." Her dad pushed the end call button on the iPhone and turned to her. "Don't ever do that to me again."

"Sorry." Alyssa took a deep breath. "She still has a hold on me. I can't stand up to her. She wanted to speak to you. I'm sorry."

"Yeah, well, please don't do that to me again." He pushed himself back up on the pillow and said, "But you can soothe my aching soul and tell me what's happening with our family."

So Alyssa told him about Haley and Travis, showed him pics on the iPhone, shared a few problems that her husband Rick was having with upper management at IBM, then told him about Sam, Glenda, and Aaron spending the week in Costa Rica with

Marion.

"Sam's there?"

She nodded.

"That's not good."

"Not to worry, Dad, he'll be calling back in five minutes, concerned that you're mad at him, too."

"Right." And then, not necessarily to her, "Talk about regrets."

"What regrets?"

"No regrets." He shook them away. "So, what about Beryl? You didn't say anything about her."

"Well...I haven't spoken with her. I kind of rushed out in a frenzy when I found the message from your 'girlfriend' on my machine. I called Sam and ran down to JFK. She just wasn't on my radar at that moment."

"Jesus Christ, Alyssa, she's your sister."

Formally chastised, Alyssa mumbled, "I'm pretty sure Mom called her. Where's your phone?"

He retrieved it from the otherwise empty drawer in the chest next to the bed and handed it over. Alyssa flipped it open and turned it on—one bar left—nine missed calls. Two from Alyssa, three from Sam, four from Beryl. "Oh yeah, she knows...she knows."

He nodded. She could tell he was still annoyed.

"So," she said, "in the four minutes we have left before Sam gets up the gumption to call you back, tell me about where you've been since I last spoke to you in New Orleans."

"I should call Beryl."

"Give me a few minutes, Dad. Please. Then we'll start taking care of business. Tell me first where you've been, where you were going when—"

And so Robert slowly recounted his solo journey from New Orleans to Lake Charles to Houston and San Antonio—where by chance he ran into Jen Magruder again, at the Smokehouse Barbecue. He paused then as if trying to remember the order in which then the two of them traveled to barbeque joints from Poteet to George West to Corpus Christi and on down to Brownsville. Then on to cantinas and enchiladas (and churos) in Monterrey, Saltillo, San Jose de Raices, Matehuala, San Luis Potosi, Querétaro, and Mexico City.

Her father's story took exactly four minutes, at which point Alyssa's phone rang. It was Sam.

Chapter Seventeen

From the queen-size bed in the back of the Winnebago, Robert could hear Alyssa and Beryl squabbling in the front of the vehicle.

He looked over at the makeshift shelf of pill bottles—Plavix, Calciparine, Lasix, Coreg, Coumadin—next to an almost-empty cup of water. Humping himself over to the edge of the mattress, he pulled the heavy curtain aside to let the sunny day inside, the sky a cloudless blue.

Then he heard Stephen Sutherland's deep voice, a rumble, and Alyssa's sharp rebuke: "This is between my sister and me, Stephen, so please let us work it out!"

Next came a long silence, then heavy footsteps, and the van door opening, slamming shut.

"What the hell is going on up there?" Robert called, gravel-voiced, swinging his feet down to the linoleum floor and reaching over to grab his robe off the hook.

"Just a friendly disagreement," Alyssa called back. "Nothing that requires intervention from a shrink."

"A friendly disagreement edging up on disagreeable," Beryl added with her mother's dryness.

By then Robert had taken the four steps necessary to make it to the kitchen area and was standing over the fold-down table where the coffee-fueled conference was taking place. He pushed his long gray hair back off his face. "Good to see my girls getting along so well! Got any coffee left for the old man?" He reached up into the small cabinet above the small sink and took out a thick and not so small Dunkin Donuts cup.

When he turned back his two daughters looked incredulous.

"What the hell is wrong with you?" they shouted, practically in unison, except Beryl appeared to use the word *fuck* instead of *hell.*

"This is not going to work," he said, reaching for a donut in the box on the table. Alyssa slapped his hand.

Beryl looked toward the door and then over at her father, "Didn't you hear one fucking word from Dr. Quintero?"

"I did," he said cheerfully.

"Then, tell me, what didn't you understand about…"—she held up one finger—"no caffeine?"—two fingers—"no salt?"—three fingers—"no junk food?"—four fingers—"lose some goddamn weight, goddamnit!?"

"And what's with that hair, Dad?" Alyssa snorted. "It's just disgusting, a man your age. I'm going to take you for a haircut today."

"This is definitely not going to work," he said, no longer smiling. "Let's get something really clear: I've been to the mountain, my dear girls, I've seen what a wretched self-righteous know-it-all creep I've been, and I'm no longer afraid to look at myself anymore. I've looked right into the maw, and I've been transformed. I am going to live for the first time in my sorry life."

Alyssa rolled her eyes at her sister. "You sound just like my last Pilates teacher."

Beryl scowled in agreement, "Well, you actually sound like the stupidest of my unbearably stupid born-again students who continue to argue that the world is 2000 years old."

He drew in a deep breath and let it out. "Well, mein wardens, I'm hungry and I'm going to have a cup of coffee and a donut, like I always do. And you two can just—"

Alyssa snatched a banana from the shelf. "Here. Take this. The doctor said you should eat potassium." Robert took the banana and dropped it into the garbage bag hanging from the shower doorknob.

By then the cabin door was open, and Stephen Sutherland was standing in a bright halo of sunlight. "Run for the hills, son," Robert growled. "These two are going to cut your balls off if it's the last thing they do!"

Stephen, doomed it seemed to always try too hard, grabbed his crotch. No one thought it was funny.

Alyssa's face showed how aghast she was before the words were out of her mouth: "I never heard you talk that way! It's appalling! I mean, what's with you, Dad? Do you have a brain tumor? Did you learn that from your skanky girlfriend?"

"Don't!" he warned, the paternal finger pointing at her nose. "And don't think you two are going to tell me where to live, what to eat, and most of all, who to sleep with!"

"Oh Jesus, Dad, please!"

Beryl's eyes widened, "Sleep with? What the—? Who the hell are you sleeping with now?"

"No one!" he screamed.

The RV grew quiet as a mausoleum. "Don't scream," Alyssa said, as calmly as if she was speaking to her five-year-old. "The doctor said things really need to be calm around here." And, turning to Beryl with a manufactured smile, "You know, he was sleeping with Ms. Over-The-Hill Skank with the dirty fingernails, the one I told you about. I thought it prudent to keep my presumptions about his carnal behavior to myself."

Beryl glanced at the door, no doubt looking for her fiancé. But the door was closed, Stephen once again gone, his feelings hurt, probably wandering around rows of tents and trailers in Campo Bucaneros on the outskirts of Mexico City.

"What's happening here?" Beryl asked, teary now. "Would one of you please tell me what's going on? What's going to happen to you?"

Robert poured himself a cup of coffee, lifted it in silent toast, and settled into the front passenger captain's chair. "I don't know, dear one," he said a little sadly. "I do know this, though: I am not going back to Elting right now, maybe ever, and the last thing you and Stephen need is a grumpy old man hanging around Asheville."

He got no resistance from Beryl, who leaned back in her chair, but Alyssa was now crying again, silently, tears slipping down her cheeks.

Robert said, "Alyssa, honey, it's got nothing to do with you. I just can't right now."

"But you could stay with us for a while—I have that room with an outside entrance. You wouldn't even have to deal with me." She stopped, a hitch in her throat. "Just for a while, until you get your meds all straightened out. Travis and Haley would love to have you around. It's almost spring and you and Rick could play some golf—and then you could head out again. I just hate to think of you driving around now all alone."

Robert sipped the black coffee. "I'm not going into details, but when I talked to your mom a few weeks ago, I learned some very unsettling things I didn't know before—and I just can't go back there now. Elting is, for lack of a better phrase, just off-limits. It's not an option. I'm sorry, sweet girl, but I'm touched you still want me around—and under different circumstances I might well have taken you up on your offer."

He was unable to resist looking over at Beryl, now holding her cup up to her lips, waiting, waiting. "What did she tell you?"

"Nothing."

"Can't be nothing. At least, let me know—"

His therapist's voice had returned. "It's nothing you need to know about—and it's got nothing to do with any of you."

"But—"

"But nothing. I know I have to figure out something. Some things. I know I can't stay here. And I know I have to find a good place to hang out for a few months, just to make sure that everything is working like it's supposed to." He pressed his lips together. "I'm really not an idiot, you know."

An hour later, when Stephen peeked his head back into the Winnebago, all three were in the same places, but now, he thought, thank God no one was yelling. In fact, the two daughters were laughing as Beryl pulled the key from the Nauset Knoll Inn from her backpack and showed it to Alyssa, who gasped and asked their dad "What the hell were you thinking? I mean, that may be the singularly most perverse thing I have ever heard of!"

"I told Beryl that—" Robert started.

Beryl made the "T" time out sign with her hands, "Oh no, I'm not sure I can do that right now. Later."

"Yeah, later," Alyssa concurred, "and maybe not in person. Maybe just in an email. I'm not sure whether I'm gonna want to laugh or puke."

"Soooo...," Stephen interrupted, "did the three of you come to some kind of agreement?"

Robert broke through the silence that followed, "No, not really."

"Nope," Beryl concurred.

Alyssa nodded, "Not really."

But they had. Robert had promised to take his medicines "religiously." He'd even agreed to be more careful about his diet. And he'd guaranteed he would see the cardiologist in two weeks for a follow-up. But there still remained the question of where he was going to live.

"Well, I can't leave here until I know what's happening with you, Dad," Alyssa muttered, and then, suddenly exasperated, reached into her jeans and pulled out the phone. "It's Sam again. I can't answer it. He's going to want to know what's happening and if I don't have an answer, this RV is going to get mighty crowded in another day." She pushed End Call.

Stephen stepped up into the RV, but stayed in the doorway after Beryl held up her hand like a traffic cop. She grew increasingly silent as it became clear to everyone that her bitchy sister Alyssa was more willing to sacrifice for their father than she. "Yeah," she said, "and unfortunately I have to get back to my classes at Wilson. My flight is tomorrow morning." She looked at her sister, "So I guess we need to figure out everything before I go."

"Oh, don't worry about that," Alyssa said, not unkindly but not kindly at all. "I'll stick around—"

Beryl was scowling. "Well, I'm not leaving until we figure everything out."

"I thought you had to leave, Beryl."

"Y'know, Alyssa—" she started but then pressed her lips together. Stephen knew enough this time around to keep his mouth shut, but he took a step over to Beryl and, standing behind her, massaged her shoulders. And for a moment she closed her eyes and leaned her head back.

So when the call came from Jen Magruder a few minutes later saying she was done working for *Lonely Planet* (she'd explain another time) and was heading for Oaxaca…and that she'd been up all night thinking about what Robert was going to do all alone in Mexcio City…and yeah, she already missed him a lot more than she thought she would…and maybe she should drive back up there after the last story was filed and the two of them maybe could spend the spring, hang out in tony Oaxaca with all the expats and their deep pockets…it was pretty much a done deal. Si?

Except for the foot-stomping tantrum that Alyssa threw when she found out he had agreed.

And the fifteen calls from Sam, each with a new suggestion regarding how and where "we can keep an eye on you."

Robert handled his two older children with the kind of grace that had escaped him while they were growing up, the kind of easy grace that was sorely misplaced all those years with his wife, the very same grace with which he was able to comfort his clients while they were tortured with anxiety—except the one time comfort turned to something else.

And when Robert said good-bye to Stephen and Beryl the next morning, Beryl stood on her tiptoes, wrapped her arms around her father's neck, and whispered "I'm sorry" in his ear.

"Right…right…right…TURN RIGHT!" Alyssa snarled, long past being sorry she'd stepped up as the good daughter, pointing out the big windshield to the exit for MEX-135D toward OAXACA/TEHUACAN. "Jesus Christ, Dad, do I have to spell out every turn for you?"

They were already four hours in to what was supposed to be a five-and-a-half-hour trip from Mexico City—and still had 200 miles to go. The imagined father-daughter bonding wasn't going well.

Robert swallowed the *Fuck you and your mother, too!* before taking a deep, cleansing breath, just like the rehabilitation specialist at ABC had told him to do when encountering stress, and said in a rather measured cadence, "I had the blinker on, Alyssa."

"Most people slow down as they approach exits," she replied, looking straight ahead.

Another deep, cleansing breath. "Well, now I'm wondering if this is the way you speak to your husband."

She laughed, "Of course not." Then she looked over at her father, a smirk flickering at the edge of his lips. "Are you asking as a psychotherapist or as the father of the daughter he drove to four years of psychotherapy and a lifetime of control issues?"

Robert was silenced, his foot pressing the gas pedal to the floor of the Winnebago as they slowly climbed another pass through the Sierra Madres. He concocted a variety of pithy responses for his snarky, mouthy, contentious daughter, but, heeding the Mexico City therapist and understanding that there was more than a scintilla of truth in her unkind accusation, he offered up his stony silence instead.

Alyssa had refused to let Robert drive to Oaxaca alone. Of course, he had resisted, insulted that she didn't think he was capable of making the trip by himself. But after Sam kept threatening to fly up and make the drive with him, Robert opted for the lesser of two agonies and let Alyssa join him. The plan was that once she left him with Jen Magruder ("...in the unwashed hands of the skank" she told her husband Tim), she would rent a car and drive straight to the Mexico City airport.

The silence felt familiar, if not comfortable, to Robert, reminiscent in so many ways of those old tight-lipped travel days with Marion in the shotgun seat of the Volvo, the two of them headed back over Mohawk Mountain, back home to Elting from the doofus marriage counselor in Stony Hills, home to Elting where, it now turned out, *my "best pal" Garrison finally got his revenge for me ending up with the better wife, the happier family, the bigger paycheck, you name it, that fuckface, fucking my fucking wife for the pure pleasure of knocking me to the goddamn fucking ground.*

"I'm not good at this," Alyssa spoke up over the whining engine and her father's silently simmering rage. "Can we call a truce, Dad? At least til we get to Oaxaca. Truce?"

Robert shrugged but held out a thick hand across the console. Alyssa held back her tears and took her father's hand. "Still swollen," she said. "A little better maybe."

He nodded. A different kind of shrug this time. "I'm always so surprised at how small and delicate your hands are."

"I've always wondered about that...I mean, you have three kids, and the big doofy, thick-handed, thick-skulled one turns out to be the son—and the two girls get to be thin and petite. What the hell is that all about? Natural selection? Luck? Is that God?"

"A couple of months ago I might have corrected you, might have asked you what you were really asking," he smiled so sadly. "I might have given you the Aetheist's Creed. But now I know that I don't know anything. So yeah, it might be God. And I guess it might not."

Chapter Eighteen

"Well, I don't think I believe in God anymore," Marion said, surprising herself and Sam, whose jaw dropped just like a good, upstanding citizen in some 1950s B-grade movie.

Leslie put her bare foot up on the rattan coffee table. "Well, it's about time you finally grew up, dear friend," she said, smiling so sweetly that Marion wondered whether she was being mocked or congratulated.

Ignoring Leslie, whom it seemed he did not like at all, Sam turned to his mother and said, "I don't think you really mean that, Mom. You've been hurt, high and low, if you get my drift, and you probably just need some time to get your sea legs back and…I don't know, set sail and…find a new path to walk on."

Marion snuck a conspiratorial look at Glenda and then laughed in spite of herself. "You're a sweet man, my Sam, and you always know what to say to make me feel better."

Sam raised his glass of wine, "To a new path…through the jungle and out of the woods." He beamed like a seven-year-old.

Marion reached for her glass of wine, "To the jungle…."

Sam, Glenda, and Aaron would be leaving Manuel Antonio the next day. After a simple dinner of mahi grilled in butter with casado and fried plantains, the four adults were sitting on the veranda, watching the sun sink and sizzle in the sliver of Pacific Ocean visible from Marion's cottage.

Glenda's face was sunburned. She raised her glass. "I'm sorry to be leaving the jungle." Then she was silent. Then "To the jungle," as she smiled and clinked glasses, first with Marion and then Sam, and then extended her glass toward Leslie, who picked up her own and said, "Let's do this right. If little else, it's what we have instead of God."

Sam scowled, his glass still in the air. "We have God, Leslie. God is with us at every single moment."

Marion appeared not to be listening.

"What I mean," Leslie continued, "is that toasting in Costa Rica is not just a convention; it has meaning. My friend Ed, hipster-surfer-shaman, told me that you need to look each other in the eye as you clink glasses so the toast actually connects the two of you. So..."

Glenda raised her glass again and looked ridiculously wide-eyed at Leslie, who opened her eyes wide in return and said, "Salud!" They clinked their glasses and moved along ritualistically to Marion, then to Sam, who reluctantly gave Leslie his eyes, who then offered his own wide-eyed "Salud!"s to Glenda and his mother.

Everyone laughed when the toasting was done, for reasons nobody really understood, and the sky grew black as the mood that had recently entered Marion's heart. Then everyone was silent, with only the rustle of monkeys moving through the trees and the whispering voice of Aaron, wandering around inside a fantasy of capturing robbers on a beach.

It appeared that they had survived the squall. Sam finished his wine and put down his glass. Marion saw him glance over at Glenda, who tilted her head, then smiled threateningly and mouthed "No!"

But, just as she knew he would, Sam broke the jungle silence like a limb cracking: "I'm sorry, but I can't believe you've lost your faith, Mother! I just don't know what to make of that..." trailing off and looking beseechingly at each of the three women in turn.

Glenda looked down into her glass of wine. Marion shook her

head. Leslie simply turned her hands over and showed him her palms. And with none of the women offering any answers or even challenges, he grabbed the bottle and poured the dregs into his empty glass.

When Marion finally spoke in the darkness of the lanai, it was a kind of long and ponderous rambling about a God that allows—"Even creates," Leslie added—abominations of the worst and most inhumane sort among his creatures.

Not to be silenced, Sam pretty much said what everyone says about faith and salvation and suffering and Almighty God's reasons for everything, "Everything," he said glaring through the darkness at Marion. Then back at Leslie. "Every single thing."

Then Leslie pretty much said what everyone says about a God who supposedly created a world full of murder, cancer, genocide, AIDS, polio, hunger, rape, madness, the hideous pain and suffering of wholesale betrayal.

Glenda sat quietly listening intently to her husband and her mother-in-law's friend talk about God. She looked across the table wondering what Marion thought of it all; and then when she could no longer hold back the tide of fury rising in her throat. "I just don't know. I don't how the two of you can be so damn sure of yourselves. You all talk like you know something. I'm going to go put that sweet boy to sleep."

"Amen," whispered Marion.

Glenda leaned over then and gave Sam a kiss on the cheek; he was stone-faced. Then around to the side of the table to hold out her hand to Leslie; then to Marion, who stood up and wept in her daughter-in-law's arms.

Chapter Nineteen

Oaxacan cuisine is varied and justifiably famous.

Or so Jen Magruder wrote first for *Cheap Eats*—and then later for *Viva Oaxaca* when she was offered a juicy contract for a whole chapter on "Fifty Oaxacan Eateries on a Budget."

Try to get in sync with local eating hours: a small breakfast, la comida, the largest meal, sometime after 2:00 p.m.; and, if you have room, a lighter cena sometime after 8:00 p.m. You'll need to request the check—"La cuenta, por favor"—and be prepared to wait for a while.

Check out La Biznaga (Garcia Vigil 512, telephone 516 1800) (between Allende and Carranza, moderately expensive), which quickly emerged as our favorite place for afternoon comida or evening cena. To start, try the sopa de fideos con chorizo, fine pasta and spicy sausage in a superb sauce.

La Biznaga was where Robert ate most meals, posing as Jen's assistant—and mostly eating for free—as an unusually cool and rainy March rolled over into the warmest April in anyone's memory.

In the two months since they'd set up housekeeping at the Oaxaca Trailer Park ("Secure Urban Camping"), Robert still hadn't shaved or cut his hair, which was now wavy and long, swept back behind his ears, flowing over his collar, nearly ponytail length. In all, he couldn't complain about an emotional state that was almost wholly alien to him for most of the first sixty years of a life lived in what Garrison, his old friend—and now mortal enemy—called Almostville. (Once, after the Tevis family returned from what had actually been a wonderful camping vacation through Bryce, Arches, and Yosemite, but with Robert carping about one thing and another, Garrison said, "Bob, you are never completely satisfied with anything. Anything. Never have been. Never will be. You, my good buddy, are doomed to be a wet blanket your whole life living in a town aptly named Almostville.")

But now he wasn't complaining. He wasn't even shrugging. Or sighing. In fact, he told Jen one evening, the two of them snuggling in bed, that he had never been happier in his whole life.

"That's ridiculous," she said, staring up at the white ceiling, her hands clasped over her breasts. "You had a life, a good life, before all this. Don't just throw all that away."

"I'm not throwing any of that away," he said, insulted but still smiling. "But you, Ms. Magruder, didn't know me before I decided to kill myself. Before I experienced my rebirth."

She laughed then, but when he turned over and pulled her toward him, slipping his hand down the back of her pajama bottoms, her soft bottom in his palm, Jen pushed back. "Whoa, big guy…you know what *su medico* had to say about that kind of stuff."

That "kind of stuff" included "lifestyle" limits on food and drink along with, worst of all, the continuing restriction on what his toothy Oaxacan physician, El Doctor Emilio Gutierrez, smilingly called "sexuales vigoroso." Robert didn't need a translator.

In truth, he'd never felt sexier in his whole life. But when Robert followed up with an awkwardly worded question about non-vigorous orgasms, the doctor sneered around his brilliantly white teeth, wagging a manicured finger at the despondent Gringo, and said simply "No."

So early every morning, Robert pretended to sleep as he snuck peeks at the lovely Jen Magruder, who tiptoed around naked and unfettered—and presumably unwatched—as she gathered up clothes for the day in order to get dressed up front. Later, when he heard the RV door shut, Robert fell back to sleep in the mordantly quiet Winnebago, bolstered by the daily belief that he would have a luscious, urgent sex dream for which he did not have to take responsibility.

It never happened.

And clearly nothing was going to happen this morning, especially after he was once again rebuked—the memory of that deliciously soft bottom still on his fingertips—when he impulsively told Jennifer that he thought he was falling in love with her, thus eliciting the second and even more emphatic "Whoa, big guy" of the morning.

"I mean, I like you, Bobby…look, I more than like you…you have to know that. But let's be real, kiddo, I'm gonna be fifty next year, and as you keep telling me, you're 'sixty fucking years old,' and the warranty is long past on both of us. I love being with you, but right now I'm happy to just be the one taking you from one place to the next. As the old song said, 'I'm your vehicle, baby, won't you hop inside my car.'"

She laughed at her own joke, but Robert lay quietly the whole time, wondering what it all meant. He'd thought he was happy. "Well," he grumbled, "I would like to hop inside your car."

Nevertheless, it was a nice easy life, he told Alyssa in measured tones on the crackly phone line the following Sunday. Dutiful as ever—and, he suspected, as annoyed as ever at her own dutifulness—she called punctually every Sunday evening and stayed on just long enough to make him promise to eat well and exercise.

It was an easy life, he assured Sam, who called more often than his sister, and who generally stayed on the line long after there was anything to say, inevitably forcing his father to make up some flimsy excuse to get off.

That was the older two. In the two months since he'd left Mexico City for Oaxaca, Beryl had called twice, both times in response to his messages, and both times they'd chatted easily about music and her recent presentation on fisher cats at an environmental conference at Warren Wilson College.

Robert even had a routine again. Around 10 a.m., he'd wake for the day, follow what Beryl had told him (and that Stephen had told her) was Robert Bly's life script of writing a poem each morning before he left the bed, then make himself some good rich Oaxaca Pluma coffee like Tres Flechas, and, travel cup in hand, set out to walk the city, dutifully fulfilling the doctor's prescription for a half hour of cardiovascular exercise. After that, because he did not have a sex dream and because there was no way that Jen or Alyssa would ever know, he'd get himself some huevos rancheros at El Sabor.

Robert was a quarter mile down the dusty road from El Sabor when he spotted the yellow and red school bus. He recognized it right away, even though it was now adorned with what appeared to be thousands of unrelated bumper stickers and decals. He walked past the restaurant and quickened his pace as he neared the bus, brimming with the utter joy of unexpected discovery.

"Bobby Fucking Bobby Bob!" Phoenix jumped out the open door, opened his arms and shouted, "You are a sight for these sore, bloodshot eyes! How goes it, my man?"

"Better!" he called back, striding up toward the bus, looking all around for Mountain Eagle and Clover. He said it in exactly the same way as he'd spoken the last time they met, as if Phoenix knew everything about the aborted suicide or the stroke or Jen Magruder…or anything else for that matter. It felt strangely like déjà vu as he approached the bus, but this was definitely not a

Wal-Mart parking lot in Asheville, North Carolina. And what's more, he was no longer the same person. The man they had known was dead.

He stood, hands at his side. For a moment then, time seemed to stand still, and Robert thought he had entered one of the lessons of Don Juan (he'd been reading Carlos Castaneda's *The Teachings of Don Juan* each night before sleep): Savannah, Mountain Eagle, and Clover appeared, swaying and now laughing in the staggering midday heat.

Robert held out his hand and Phoenix ignored it, wrapping his long arms around the older man's shoulders, the others crowding around and yipping like desert dogs. They stunk, but it did not matter. When Phoenix let him go, Clover leaped into his arms and held him tighter than any human being had ever squeezed him before. Two, three, four, five seconds passed before he realized she was sobbing.

"What's wrong, sweetheart?"

"It's so wrong, so fucking wrong!" she finally gasped, barely able to catch her breath.

"Tell me," he cooed.

"The fucking Federales!" growled Phoenix from behind, "The pigs ripped up the bus, stole our dope, and took all our cash!"

Robert gently unleashed Clover's arms from his neck. "The police stole your money?"

She nodded, her cheeks stained with tears, and crisscrossed with the imprint of his shirt. She was trembling. "All of it," she said.

He turned to the others. "When did this happen? Did you call the embassy?"

Mountain Eagle tilted his shaggy head and took a deep breath. Robert instantly felt stupid. "I'm sorry. I am sorry," taking his own deep breath now. "Tell me, tell me...when did all this happen?"

"Three-four days ago," said Mountain Eagle, the passion gone from his voice. "We're still trying to figure out what we're going to do."

"Have you eaten?"

No one said a word. "Not since yesterday morning," Savannah finally spoke just above a whisper, looking right and left at the boys. "That was the last of the rice and oatmeal."

Robert walked over to the bus then, stepping up and grabbing onto the chrome rail and hoisting himself into what he described to Jennifer later that day as "utterly rank and disgusting" (She'd laughed, saying "You don't know disgusting or rank, Bobby."): clothes and dishes and newspapers strewn all over the place, posters ripped from the walls, torn curtains, the mattress knifed open, stuffing like intestines coming up through the gashes. The place reeked of sweat and moldy food and beer and pot.

When he turned around, they were right behind. "Man, this place stinks!" he said, pushing them down the steps and out the door. He took a deep breath to clear the stench in his nostrils. "I'm going straight to the consulate."

"That's not a good idea, Bobby," Mountain Eagle said, his arm around Clover's shoulders. "You'll just be making more trouble for us—and maybe yourself. You have to know there are some really mean dudes around here."

"No, I mean the American Consulate. They'll be able to help."

Mountain Eagle glanced around at his friends.

Phoenix was now shaking his head. "I don't like it," he said.

Savannah spoke then: "Maybe, y'know, if you could maybe lend us a few bucks to get through—"

Phoenix cut in, "Yeah, just enough money for some oil for the bus, so we can make it to the coast and get some hotel jobs. We'll pay you back, Bob. I promise." And you know…," he smiled.

Clover and Mountain Eagle, obviously embarrassed, looked down at their shoes. Robert nodded and turned their way. "We'll figure it out," he said waiting for Clover to raise her eyes to meet his. "In the meantime, you all must be starving. Let's grab some *jamón y huevos* at El Sabor and talk it over. You all need some protein," he added, surprising himself with the authority gained with his new nutritional regimen.

Clover left the shelter of Mountain's arm and hugged Robert again. Then he was hugged by Savannah. Then by Mountain Eagle, who whispered in his ear, "You're a righteous dude, Bobby." He looked like a little boy then. Only Phoenix stood back.

"You also reek, all of you," Robert said without rancor. "I don't think I can take you into a restaurant smelling like this." He looked around at the four of them, who suddenly appeared to him as the ragamuffin children they were—even Phoenix, swaying now like a mangy cur outside the pack.

Phoenix lifted his arm and sniffed deeply and loudly, already coughing out that tobacco laugh at his own impending joke, "Mmmmm, I love the smell of asshole in the morning."

"Take off your shirts," Robert said, pointedly ignoring the boy's obvious attempt to rattle him. "And find something, anything, that doesn't stink in all this mess to put on."

All four lifted their shirts over their heads like toddlers getting ready for a bath, the two bony-chested boys stepping back up into the bus and clomping around, the two perky-breasted girls bent over with their bare arms pressed against themselves as they rummaged around in the mess for something to cover themselves, something he hoped didn't reek so badly.

Then they followed him like ducklings down the road to a small *tienda*, where he told them to wait outside while he bought a handful of deodorants and passed them around.

Robert stood on the cracked concrete sidewalk and watched

the four of them slather themselves up and down, up and down. "One more time," he said, until they all smelled of an odd and not totally unpleasant combination of patchouli, Old Spice, and ordinary BO. He felt content for the first time since the morning discussion with Jen.

And an hour later, bellies full and now looking and smelling like a pack of mangy defumigated dogs, the unlikely group stepped out of El Sabor into the blindingly bright midmorning sun—orange circles pulsing in their squinting eyes—when Clover cried out, "The bus is gone!"

The four young people ran down the dusty road to the empty spot where it had been parked, arms flapping pointlessly up and down like flightless birds, each turning around and around in some kind of hapless dance, hands shielding their eyes, searching for the forty-foot vehicle that had simply disappeared into the shimmering hot air. Breathing in and out through his nose like an enraged bull, Robert followed behind.

———————————

Jen turned her back on him, glaring through the small jalousie window at the four dirty hippies waiting in the dust outside the Winnebago. "What the hell are you thinking, Bob? We don't have room here...."

"They're just kids, they don't have a pot to piss in."

"Bob," she said, watching Mountain Eagle do a weird dance with his Rasta hacky sack, "those kids haven't pissed in an actual pot in years, but they've somehow managed to keep themselves fed and high and dry all this time. They'll be all right. They know how to survive."

He shook his head and reached for the cup of coffee on the small table, his fourth of the day. "They have nowhere to go, Jen. We walked out of El Sabor, and the bus was gone. What was I supposed to do?"

"Show them the way to the homeless shelter."

"I can't do that. It's a dangerous place. I read about it in the *Oaxaca Times*."

"What do you think, they're gonna get robbed? Of what? Truth is, you're the one who's gonna get himself shanked and robbed, Bobby boy. You're a sweet guy, this new you, but you got a lot to learn."

He glared at her. "They're sweet kids, Jen—back in Virginia, they could've dumped me on the side of the road and made off with this RV. I told you all about that."

"You told me about those two," nodding over at Mountain Eagle and Clover, "and I guess I can see some sweetness in them, especially the girl. But I'd imagine that one"—she pointed at Phoenix, hands on his hips, just staring out into the hazy distance—"has done his own share of mean, nasty stuff along the way, and he'd just as soon stick a rusty knife in your belly as sweet-talk you, if it made it easier to take your wallet."

Robert sat down at the folding table, his chest heaving in anger. "I didn't realize you were so cynical."

She turned around, reaching over to lift his chin between thumb and forefinger, "I didn't realize you're so damn naïve, Bobby boy. What were you thinking all those years, sitting across from rich people pouring out their guts? Didn't you listen to them, or did you just take their money?"

"It wasn't like that, Jen." His face was red now. He gulped down the last inch of coffee and reached for the pot.

"You've had enough," she scolded. "The doctor—"

"Fuck the doctor," he yelled, "and...fuck you, you're not my wife!"

Her eyes grew wide, her face white with a different kind of rage than his. She muttered to herself, "That's right, Dr. Tevis, I'm not your fucking wife." And with that, she turned, took two strides back toward the bed and began stuffing her clothes strewn all around into the big backpack leaning in the corner. "And I'll tell you what, Jack," she continued, bent over the backpack, needlessly unzipping and zipping the pockets, "I don't need this shit. I don't need to be taking care of an invalid. I actually thought you were different than all the other assholes I've known, grown men who can't wipe their own asses, pathetic little boys who beat the shit out of women and then weep like babies."

She paused, still bent over the backpack, thumb and forefinger holding tight to a zipper pull, as if waiting for his response.

When it didn't come, when Robert grimly picked up the coffee pot, silenced in the face of another woman walking out on him, she repeated herself, softer now, a tremor in her voice, "I got my own problems, Bobby, I don't need to be taking care of an invalid."

It was as if the world stopped spinning on its axis in that moment, a game of statues in process: Jen bending over the backpack, no voices outside the window, no flies buzzing inside the motor home, no hum from the air conditioner, and Robert feeling more than hearing glass shattering, shards flying, the hot liquid splattering across the linoleum, himself falling with a thump to the wet floor.

Chapter Twenty

"Take this, Bobby." In her upturned palm, Jennifer Magruder held a small paper cup.

Robert shifted himself in the wheelchair and held out his right hand, the other folded inconsequentially in his lap. He took the cup and slid the pills through his slanted lips.

Taking the empty cup with one hand, she held out a larger cup and straw with the other. "And please fucking swallow them this time!"

He nodded and smiled a crooked smile back at her, the first glimmer of any kind of happiness that cold morning, his grim blue eyes watching her move effortlessly around the white room.

"Okay," she said. turning to the open suitcase on the hospital bed, placing the pillbox in the satin inside pocket, closing the lid, and zipping it shut around two rounded corners. "I think we're all set, Bobby."

He nodded.

She pulled a black sketchbook from her bolsa, opened it, and scanned a few pages, slipping a pen out from its niche above her ponytail and checking off one, two, three final items on her list. "So, everything is good…meds are in the suitcase, and the speech therapy instructions are in this looseleaf"—which she grabbed off the unmade hospital bed—"along with all the info the good Dr. Gutierrez left for you."

He nodded.

"So…are you ready to hit the highway, old man?"

He nodded again. The man she knew a few months ago was still sunk deep behind those pleading eyes. She said nothing, but was pleased to see the left side of his face gaining back some muscle tone.

She handed him the standard-issue metal cane. Turning to another page in the journal, she said, "Okay, let's review what we know: Clover and Mountain Eagle should be waiting for you in the lobby. They'll drive you down to San Jose. In that tin crate on those cattle path roads, the drive should take at least a week—or more. You got that, Bobby?"

He nodded.

"When you're a day away, you'll call Alyssa. She and Sam will be waiting for you in San Jose. Then they'll drive with the three of you down to Manuel Antonio. Got it, Bobby?"

He wouldn't look at her.

"Got it?"

He took a deep breath, nodded, and stuck out his tongue.

"Good! Now you're a five-year-old. You know, hotshot, Marion, who I've come to understand pretty well over the past three months, was far too good for you." She paused just long enough for Robert to crack the second crooked smile of the day and give her the finger with his still-strong right hand. "Marion has her hacienda all tricked out for you. Beryl will be down in a few weeks."

His head was now bobbing up and down in anticipation of each incoming demand, making her wonder if he was even listening to what she was saying.

"What else? Do you have your notebook? Your address book? The cell phone? The doctor's card? The name of that witch doctor down in Quepos? Your cane? Do you really think you're ready for all this?"

He glared at her.

"What?"

He shook his head.

"Talk to me, Bobby. I know you can do it. Clover told me this morning that you can say—"

He was still glaring at her, his hair long enough now to be swept back into a ponytail, one slim weave with a bead made by Clover behind his left ear. "Clover said you're making real progress. She said—"

He growled then and pointed to the notebook in her hand.

"Talk to me, Bobby. We gotta start somewhere."

Robert jutted his jaw and jabbed his index finger once through the antiseptic air. Then again.

It was she who nodded then, "Okay, okay…," turning the page in the book and laying it in his lap. Robert flopped the limp hand over the top of the pages to hold them down and took the pen in the other. He clicked the pen twice on his shoulder and then wrote: I AM NOT A FUCKING IDIOT!

She reached over and placed her palm on his cheek. "Oh, I beg to differ, Bobby boy, you are one big fucking idiot. A goddamn big one. And frankly I have no idea why the hell I'm still hanging around with you. I should've been gone a long time ago—months ago. I am, if you hadn't noticed, free, white and forty-nine with a sweet little ass."

He wrote: YOU'RE THE IDIOT.

And crooked smile number three slipped out as he added: BUT YOU DO HAVE A VERY NICE ASS.

She shook her head and bent over the man, placing her lips over his, soft and lingering, her hand cupping his ear, her tongue barely touching his. She stood then, wiping a tear from the corner of her eye. "You're right, Herr Doctor, I am the idiot. I should see a shrink."

Smile number four.

Then Jennifer Magruder, Freelance Food Writer and Low Rent Bon Vivant (as it said on her business card), walked around behind the shiny wheelchair, stepped on the brake pedal to release it, and pushed Robert down the long hallway to the elevator.

"I'll be down in Manuel Antonio in six weeks," she said, "and then I guess we'll see what we got."

———————

"We've got a full house," Marion said, not unkindly, handing two fruity-looking cocktails to the smiling young hippies who had just driven Robert all the way from Oaxaca down to San Jose and then Quepos. "I'm really sorry to ask you, especially after all you've done for Robert, but would it be all right if you two stayed in the camper for a few days?"

The kids were on the veranda, sipping their sweet rum concoctions with Alyssa, Sam, and Marion's friend Leslie. Robert was asleep in the bedroom Marion had fixed up for him. Despite what she had been assured to be Clover's loving attentiveness and Mountain Eagle's indulgent driving skills, the two-week ramble over rough Mexican and rougher Costa Rican roads had left Robert weary beyond weary.

Mountain Eagle glanced at Clover, who opened her eyes wide, a surprised smile flickering on her lips.

"We thought—" she began and stopped.

"We thought," Mountain Eagle continued for her, "that you were just going to pay us and send us packing." He snickered like a young foal.

"Oh no!" Marion said. "No, not at all. We want you to stay...I know that Robert really wants you to stay. He's grown very fond of you two, you know—and he needs you right now." She then turned to her silent children. "I mean, right? That's what Jennifer told us on the phone."

Sam shrugged. Alyssa pressed her lips together and nodded.

Leslie leaned back on the floral couch and smiled knowingly when Alyssa put her drink on the coaster, stood up, and excused herself.

Turning to the two hippies sitting at the edge of the rattan chairs, Marion said, "Of course, that's only if you can stick around for a while. I mean, I don't know if you have plans…"—Sam's cough filled the pause before she continued— "…or whether you need to get going, I mean, you know, somewhere else or, I don't know, and here I am just babbling along—" at which point Leslie laughed out loud at Marion stumbling through the niceties.

"Ignore my friend, please," Marion scolded. "What I mean is, do you two want to stick around and attend to Robert or do you have to get back on the road? And"—glancing at Sam's sneer—"please know that both of you are welcome here for as long as you would like to stay."

"Cool," Mountain Eagle said, quickly picking up his glass and taking one, then a second, sip. "Thank you."

"Does that mean you're staying?" Leslie asked, still leaning back on the sofa, one arm up on the pillow.

Clover nodded, tight little nods, as if she might burst into tears…or song. "We'd really like to if it's okay with everyone. Y'know, we've really gotten tight with, um—"

Alyssa reappeared in the open doorway. "So, yeah, what exactly are your plans?"

Clover looked at Alyssa, arms on either side of the doorway like some kind of giant parrot leaning onto the veranda, and cleared her throat. Then she looked at Mountain. Then Marion. "Well, we thought you wouldn't want us around, so we were just going to leave, but, um, like I said I've, we've really gotten pretty tight with, um, Bobby"—Sam coughed again—"and, y'know, I've been working with him on his speech. The doc back in Oaxaca gave me exercises to do with him every day—and, man, he's doing really, y'know, well, really well…and then Mountain, he's been following the doc's orders about his physical therapy and that's going pretty well, too." Beads of sweat had formed on her forehead and her eyes were now trained on Mountain Eagle. "I mean, you shoulda seen him a few weeks ago, before we got him up on the cane. So, yeah…I guess, we'd really like to stay around."

By then Marion was glowering at Alyssa, who ignored her, instead staring blankly out into the jungle. "So it's settled, you two stay around as long as you want…as long as Robert wants." Her eyes shifted to Leslie. "I really don't think I'm the one to be doing therapy with him."

Leslie guffawed at that, reaching over to the table to pick up her glass and raise it in the warm humid air. "Well, here's to getting the good doctor well and outa here!"

Marion grew teary then and raised her glass toward the chirping wilderness.

Leslie gently inserted the words of Marion's wordless cheer: "Hear, hear!" Sam raised his glass chin high. Alyssa thrust out an empty hand. Mountain lifted up the empty glass that he had just drained. And Clover wept.

———————

And so it went that night—and the next several days—one beautiful sunny day made different from the others only by what they ate for dinner, one evening cooked by Marion, the next by Leslie, the next some kind of jungle-looking dark orange root stew Mountain Eagle prepared while Alyssa and Sam went out to dinner in Manuel Antonio.

By the time Alyssa and Sam were only a few days away from returning home to Elting, Robert had made what appeared to be remarkable progress, both in his speech and in his ability to walk around with the aid of his cane. Everyone was pleased and relieved, of course, especially Alyssa and Sam, who wanted to get home. Only Clover and Mountain Eagle knew that the trip down through the jungle had been so hot and miserable that Robert had only recovered back to the level he had attained back in Oaxaca before they left.

Mountain Eagle explained to Marion how each morning he would follow Jen Magruder's "model" from back in Oaxaca; he would push, badger, cajole, and finally demand that Robert complete every one of his prescribed arm, leg, and facial exercises. And after lunch on the veranda and a nap, Clover would work gently and insistently on his withered left arm and on his speech. "Say it for me, Poppy" became her mantra, Mountain said, first as a joke and then later, without either of them noticing, not a joke at all.

Over those long languid days, when Marion, Alyssa, and Sam—already growing a bit weary of each other—had little to do except lie around, read some magazines, and go to the beach, it became clear to Marion that Clover, her tattoos and dreds notwithstanding, had won over Sam. He perked up when she walked into the room, talked earnestly about the benefits of yoga and organic foods, and grew animated one night over dinner as he described the scene at "Woodstock 25"—as he called it—up in Saugerties. All the while, Alyssa rolling her eyes at her brother for making a fool of himself.

One morning, after they watched Clover work with Robert in the shade of a palm tree, Sam confided to Marion and Alyssa, "She really is amazing with the old man. I mean, she's so patient and sweet—and I don't think I've ever seen him so, I don't know, relaxed?"

Alyssa blew the humid air out of her lungs. She'd confided in Marion that she wasn't taken with the girl as Sam was, but had chosen to ignore what she'd come to understand as her brother's stunning naïveté and potentially gross crush on a young girl. Now she reluctantly admitted, "He seems to like her, I guess— and yes, I can understand his speech much better now, though I suspect a lot of that is just getting used to hearing him stutter."

"Well, whatever it is, she's a godsend," Marion said, looking around to make sure they were alone. "And frankly, so is her very weird and rather skinny friend, Mr. Eagle."

All three laughed at that and then again, when she added in a whispery growl, "He's so sweet. I just wish he didn't stink so much."

"Whew! That boy could stink up a locker room," Sam said too loudly, smirking at his own witty turn of phrase.

She hushed him, her finger over her lips.

"Clover doesn't smell, though," he added in a whisper.

Alyssa shook her head in disgust. "You're getting worse than the old perv out there," pointing out to the tree where Robert was practicing "O" sounds. "Anyway, she doesn't seem to know her boyfriend has BO—or maybe she just doesn't mind? In any case, those two kids really love each other."

Sam nodded. His voice was just above a whisper now, "You know, Alyssa, you're the real perv, thinking those things." She stared at him like he was a moron, like she did when they were teenagers. "Anyway, he seems to really like her. Dad, I mean. And Clover, she seems very attached to him. Those were real tears when you told her they could stay in the camper."

Neither said a word, so he asked, "Either of you know anything about how they met Dad?"

Marion shrugged. Alyssa changed the topic altogether: "Mom, when did you say Beryl was coming?"

"Next week, Tuesday." She turned to Sam. "That should be pretty interesting, hmmm?"

"Sorry I'm gonna miss it," Sam said sincerely.

"Not me," countered Alyssa. "It could get pretty bloody. Or, on second thought, maybe I *am* sorry I won't witness the tornado that's coming the old man's way." She laughed.

Marion laughed, too. "You are awful!"

"Well, I learned from the best, Mom." Alyssa turned to Sam, "So what's up for the last dinner—it's our turn, right?"

Sam had that old look on his face like he knew there was a trap in there somewhere, but couldn't at the moment find out where it was. He just shrugged.

"I'm thinking takeout from El Mirador or maybe we'll all go down to Barba Roja's—I like the monkeys down there."

Marion bit into her lower lip. "If we do that, I guess someone will have to tell Eagle boy that he needs to shower?"

Alyssa stiffened. "Oh no, we don't have to take them, do we?"

"How can we not? We've all been together this week—and your father, well he's—"

"He's smitten with her, the old goat. I mean, let's be honest, Mom. This whole thing has been about him rediscovering some fantasy hippie past—the long hair, the van, that awful woman in Mexico City, these kids. It's kind of pathetic. Besides, I don't want to pay for them."

Sam's round face grew red. "Well, I think the jury's out on both of them. Anyway, I'll pay for her, I mean them."

———————

That afternoon, after Sam had watched Mountain finish a particularly frustrating physical therapy session where Robert resisted every one of his instructions...after the six of them had shared a silent lunch of rice and beans and some re-heated chicken and fried plantains...after his father had retired for his nap...after Clover and Mountain Eagle had left for the beach...

after his mother had left for the *mercado*…only then were he and Alyssa finally alone on the veranda.

He waited until the puttering of Marion's Toyota was absorbed into the jungle noises, then turned to his sister: "What do you think about Mom and Leslie? I mean, do you think Mom's a—"

"A dyke?" She grinned.

"You're so damn crude, Alyssa…I meant, do you think she's having a relationship with Leslie?"

"You meant dyke, big brother, but no matter. So…," rubbing her chin like some vaudevillian, "do I think she's a lesbian?" She paused, "No. Uh-uh."

Sam grimaced and a few seconds later righted his face. Then he said, "Really? You really don't think that she and Leslie have those kind of feelings for—"

"Really, Sam. The woman ran off with Pastor Smiley Face, didn't she?"

He nodded.

Alyssa offered a taunting pat on his shoulder. "Though I have to say I always thought he was gay. Live and learn, right?"

Sam leaned on the rail. "That's a relief."

"That she's not a dyke?"

He flinched. "Yeah, I guess so."

"I may be crude, Sam, but you're an infant sometimes. What would it matter if Mom is a lesbian?"

"I'm just uncomfortable with that idea—is that all right? I don't want my mother—" He didn't finish the sentence.

"It's fine with me, wallow in your little boy discomforts, but I didn't say she wasn't fooling around with Ms. Leslie, I just said she wasn't a hardcore lesbian."

"Oh Jesus, Alyssa!"

"And what are you 'oh Jesusing' about?" It was their father, standing in the opened sliding glass doorway, enunciating each word just as Clover had coached him.

"How long have you been standing there?" demanded Alyssa.

"Why aren't you sleeping, Dad?" Sam asked. "Is something wrong? Are you okay?"

He took a deep breath and began again, one word at a time: "Well, the two of you pretty much sum it up, don't you? Textbook. I think that's why I got out of the psychotherapy racket—after we're all talked out, it's pretty much a matter of birth order and genetics."

Alyssa raised her eyebrows. "Not that I haven't said that all along. And just for the record, that's not why you quit your practice. Anyway, how long were you standing there spying on us?"

"I didn't hear anything you didn't want me to hear. And," turning to Sam, "yes, son, I'm absolutely fine. Thank you."

"Then what are you doing out of bed?"

Leaning heavily on his cane, his dad limped onto the veranda and lowered himself down into one of the wicker chairs. He looked first at Sam, then at Alyssa. "I only tell them I'm taking a nap. Usually I read or listen to music—" He pulled a Walkman out of his breast pocket. "The truth is I just need to get away from your mother for a few hours."

"Oh?" asked Alyssa.

"No big deal...nothing diabolic, nothing terribly complicated—I'm just done with that part of my life—and so is she, for that matter. Frankly, there's just so much togetherness that either of us can stand. So I take an afternoon 'nap' every day." He smiled that crooked smile that had hung around after his face had regained its symmetry.

"But—"

"But nothing, Sam. Did you think your mother and I would miraculously be reconciled by this goddamn stroke—and be one big, happy family again?"

Sam shrugged. "I just thought, you know, that sometimes circumstances allow us to reconcile the past."

"Well, I'm sorry, but you thought wrong, son. I don't mean to sound harsh, but while I still have great affection for your mother—and you know that I do—but that ship sailed long ago."

"But you have so much history together—and don't you still share the love you once...?"

"Oh, Sammy," he said, shaking his head dolefully. "I do love your mother in some odd way, the way you love your arm after it's essentially useless." He picked up his left arm by the wrist and let it drop. "But we've both moved on. Don't get me wrong, she's a damn good person, your mother, especially when she's not angry at someone, but don't fool yourselves by this arrangement, she's doing all this for the three of you—and mostly you two—not for me."

Sam suddenly realized that Alyssa was unusually silent, turning to the couch where she sat red-faced, tears flowing down her cheeks. He made a move to sit down next to her, but she waved him off.

"I'm okay, " she said. "Just give me a minute, okay?"

Sam held up his hands and nodded, then ambled over to the rail. From his new vantage point, he was somewhat horrified to see his father begin struggling to raise himself out of the cushioned chair. He resisted the urge to rush over and help as his dad, his hand shaking on his cane, bore down, lifted up his bulk, and made his way across the veranda to the couch, where he slumped down next to Alyssa, leaning his weak side into her shoulder.

"I'm sorry, baby girl," he said. "I didn't know you thought this was something else." He paused before adding, "I guess that's another sign that I should have gotten out of the business a long time ago."

Alyssa smiled so sadly then, more tears trickling down her

cheeks before she leaned her head on her father's shoulder. "I don't know what I thought," she said in a thick, soft voice. "I just want things like they used to be, that's all. I'm just being selfish."

"Well, let me show you two something before the rest of them get back here." He held out his good hand for Sam to pull him up, then led the two of them haltingly out of the house, down the short dirt driveway and into the road—up the hill maybe fifty healthy paces (a hundred limping) and then left down a narrow path carved into the thick forest.

"Where are we going?" Alyssa said, looping her hand around her father's weak arm.

"Just up around this bend." He pointed the cane. "You'll see."

"I don't think he should be walking around like this," Sam said from behind. "This is rough terrain."

His dad stopped and, leaning on the cane, turned to him and growled, "Don't talk about me as if I'm not here!"

He held his hands up in surrender. Alyssa, looking over her shoulder, made a gun of her thumb and forefinger and popped Sam, blowing away the imaginary smoke with a smile.

"Okay. Now that we've got that settled, let's get where we're going. It's not too far."

Moments later, they came to a sunny green clearing with a small cabin up on short pilings. It had a red tin roof, a front porch that ran the length of the building, and two small windows on either side of a yellow door.

His father stopped and, shifting the cane from good hand to bad and leaning heavily on Alyssa, dug deep in his pocket for a green and white lanyard with a skeleton key dangling from the big metal clip at the end.

"Hey," Alyssa laughed. "I made that thing for you at camp a hundred years ago! There's the Chinqueka 'C' on the clip!"

"Yes, you did—and it's been sitting in my glove box—several

glove boxes actually—waiting for the right key." He held it up like it was the key to the gates of heaven.

"What is going on, Dad?" Sam demanded.

His father smiled his crooked smile. "I rented this pile."

"Pile?" Alyssa said. "You've been reading too many detective books. This is not a pile, it's a shack."

"Shack, pile, cabin, sanctuary, call it whatever you want, sweet Alyssa, I rented it and I'll be moving in next week with my 'handlers,' Clover and Mountain Eagle. And if it turns out I like living here, I might even buy it. That's part of the deal."

"What deal?"

"The deal I made with myself a few months before this goddamned stroke brought me down," he said, a little mysteriously. "In any case, I can't—I won't—live with your mother anymore. And don't fool yourselves, she needs to get me out of her house." Then he winked: "This way, I'll be close enough to keep an eagle eye on her and her girlfriend."

Alyssa groaned, a mock groan.

Sam was already on the front porch, trying to turn the door handle. The lanyard hit him in the middle of his back.

Chapter Twenty-One

Jed Blackstone sat on a boulder behind the small Manuel Antonio New Day Church, wiping sweat off his brow with his forearm. It had been a whole morning of moving rocks, making a wall at the back end of the property for no good reason that he could see. Just one more seemingly arbitrary chore created by Pastor Henriquez, who always looked crisp and cool in his white linen shirts; who always said with a smile, "It's good for your soul, Jedidiah." And always repeated, "Good for your soul, son."

By mid-June, Jed had whitewashed the church inside and out, re-roofed the addition, constructed rails around the back deck, built a fence for the vegetable garden, planted annuals along the pathway up to the entrance of the small sanctuary and, using hurricane clamps, steadied the big cross attached to the peak of the building.

Once, as Jed looked down from the roof of the building while painting the back of the cross and saw the Pastor lie down in a hammock strung between two massive palm trees, he called out angrily, "I finally get it, Mr. Miyagi! I finally see what's happening here!"

The Pastor looked perplexed. "Come down out of the sun, Jedidiah!" he called across the lawn. "I think you're getting sunstroke. Put the paint away. You can finish up later."

Another time, while whitewashing the fence around the tiny graveyard, Jed looked up to see the Pastor climbing into the rusted Chevy '86 Impala in the shed, cranking up the old beast and backing it out onto the new mowed lawn, braking hard just before plowing into the fence. "Hey!" Jed yelled, "you're gonna bust my fence!"

Henriquez leaned out the window. "Not even close," he said with a twinkle in his dark as coal eyes. "Besides, it's not your fence, it's mine." Then, squinting into the sun, he pointed to the paint can and made up and down painting motions with his hand.

Jed laughed. "Right," he said, and making opposite circles in the air with his hands, he called out "Wax on. Wax off!"

The Pastor shrugged, copied the motion with his left hand, and with the right on the big silver knob on the steering wheel, turned the big car off onto the pebble driveway and clear out of sight, all the way muttering to himself, "All those crazy Americans that show up here."

Despite their proximity—no more than two miles from Pastor Henriquez's parsonage to Marion's turquoise-painted home in the hills—and the small population of Manuel Antonio, Jed and Marion had never run into each other since the day he—full of the shame of nakedness before man and God, and reeking of the stink of self-loathing, unfolded himself from the Corolla—had closed the door behind him even as Marion was grinding the gears and lurching off in a cloud of red dust.

That was four months ago. So on a Saturday morning in late June, when Marion stopped by the Supermercado in Quepos, Jed Blackstone was not among the many thoughts marauding through her overactive mind. She was at the market to pick up dinner for Beryl's arrival, which had already been postponed three times over the last two months. Once because Beryl was "furious" at her father, then again, for a letter he wrote trying to explain—and atone for, he said—why he had the affair with Brenda Holloway. Then later, during a bout with the flu when Beryl was advised to stay away from her ailing father until she was better.

And yet there he was, Jed, basket slung over his forearm, staring into the dairy case as if there were momentous decision to be made. Marion's instinct was to turn around and hide in the next aisle (and maybe leave the mercado altogether and drive around the hills for a half hour or so, returning to her shopping only when he would be safely gone). But she couldn't take her eyes off of him, tan and, yes, even muscular, sinewy triceps as he reached into the case and picked up two pints of what looked like ice cream.

He was so focused on the choices at hand that he didn't notice Marion moving closer, nor when she tilted her head to better read the labels on the containers. "Personally, I'd go with the real ice cream," she said with a smile. "That frozen yogurt won't—"

He jumped, eyes wide.

"It looks like you've lost some weight, Jeddy. You could use a little fat in your diet."

He smiled, but it was not a smile of happiness—or relief—more like a man caught in a wind tunnel. "Marion…," he finally spoke.

"Yep. It's me, not a ghost."

"I'm sorry." He shook his head. "I just wasn't—I mean I just wasn't expecting to see you…and I was so consumed by this silly decision."

She nodded, resisting the temptation to touch his smooth arm.

"Long time," he said.

She didn't know why, but all she could think to say in her soft singsong voice was, "One too many mornings…and a thousand miles behind."

He tilted his head.

"Dylan," she said.

"Before my time."

"I know." She breathed in deeply. "Maybe that was at the heart of the problem."

Then there was silence, two figures in a dimly lit Edward Hopper painting that never made it to the canvas.

"Marion," he said finally. She looked up. "I don't know what to say. I'm just so…I don't know."

"Don't say anything, Jeddy," she whispered, tears forming in the corners of her eyes. She lifted her hand to his cheek, stood as tall as she could on her tiptoes, and kissed him softly on his willing lips.

But when he dropped the containers into the basket and reached over for her shoulder, she pulled back. "No," shaking her head and wiping back the tears with her index finger. "No."

"Can I call you?" he asked.

She looked straight into his glistening eyes. "No." But when she saw his countenance drop, she relented, "I don't know, Jed. Call me in a few weeks and then we'll see."

He swallowed. "I'll call. Not for anything. Just to talk about, you know, everything that happened."

"Don't call this week."

He tilted his head.

"Beryl's coming in."

He nodded and, with nowhere else to turn, glanced down into the basket as if to resume the pointless pondering over ice cream and frozen yogurt.

When he looked up again, still having made no decision, Marion was at the end of the aisle where she regained her voice. "Take the ice cream, Jed. You could use a few pounds."

———————

Robert scowled at Clover, strawberry dreds framing the long Modigliani face as she exaggerated her mouth movements reciting, "Peter Piper picked a peck of pickled peppers—" She stopped abruptly. "Please don't give me that look, Bobby. You know the drill. Now…Peter Piper picked a peck of pickled peppers…come on, Bobby!"

Robert pressed his lips together as if he was going to push out the *P*, then shook his head and stared blankly out over the dense jungle. An iguana scampered under the porch. "I'm done," he said.

She looked at her Mickey Mouse wristwatch, a present from Jen Magruder before they left for Manuel Antonio. "Un-uh, Bobby, we still got fifteen minutes." She held up her arm awkwardly so he could look at the big dial. "Dr. Gutierrez said we have to do the full hour—"

Robert stood up with a groan, leaned sideways on the cane. "Nope. I'm done." He smiled, then held the cane up in the air like a baton and, without warning, whipped it out over the railing, spinning end over end into the tiny front yard. Both of them watched open-mouthed as the cane bounced out to the base of a tree where it came to rest among broken palm fronds. A green iguana skittered across the overgrown grass. Then Robert reached into his shorts pocket, took out two vials of pills, held them up in the air like a clay pigeon, and tossed the pair over the rail, bouncing on the thick grass.

Clover leaped off the small porch and ran barefoot to retrieve the two vials. When she turned back, Robert was standing, swinging open the screen door with his weak hand and ambling into the cottage.

"Okay," she yelled from the grass, running and leaping up the three steps to the porch and following him into the small house. "So we'll just pick up tomorrow where we left off today. I'll add fifteen minutes to the exercises." Her voice trailed off. She had long since given up trying to bully the man into doing his exercises like she had seen Jen Magruder do back in Oaxaca. If he was afraid of nothing else in this world, as she'd told Eagle a few days before, the man was big-time afraid of that woman.

Not her.

Robert turned then, the scowl gone from his tanned face. Now just sadness remained in the lines around his squinting eyes. "No, sweet girl, I mean I'm d-d-d-done with speech therapy. I've had it."

"But we—"

"But nothing." The scowl was back. "I'm finished. I can talk. I can talk as good as I'm ever going to be able to talk ever again. You d-d-did a great job. And I'm very thankful. You deserve a big fat gold medal for putting up with me. But, please forgive my French, this Peter Piper shit is just goddamn humiliating...and now I'm done."

Clover reached over and took his weak hand, pressed the back of it to her cheek. "Oh Bobby, just two more weeks," she pleaded, forcing a smile onto her face. "We'll switch out Peter Piper for something else, I don't know, maybe some Dylan lyrics or something. Let's just carry on for two more weeks and Jen will be here—and then maybe we can—"

"Yeah, Jen, that's all I need right now."

"She can explain better than I can," Clover pleaded.

"No!" he snapped, using his shoulder to yank his hand from her grasp. "I have today come as far as I'm ever going to come. Time to face facts. I am not getting any better."

"That's not true!" tears filling her eyes, "We're still making good progress every day—"

"Bullship!" He gritted his teeth. "I mean bull shit! Bull shit!"

"Mountain!" she cried.

Then she screamed, "Mountain!!"

Mountain Eagle, who was behind the cottage setting up for the afternoon physical therapy session, swooped in through the kitchen door, mouth open, face white with fear.

"Tell him he can't quit!" she sobbed.

Mountain looked at Robert, who had already turned his back on him. "Bobby Bob, wassup, bro?" He moved toward the older man, reached up and put his oversized hands on his shoulders, smiling first, then kneading and kneading and kneading the slope of skin and muscle down his neck, "We can skip the session today—I'm cool with that. I'm cool with that. It's all good," kneading and kneading some more.

"It's not today he's quitting!" Clover cried, suddenly furious with Mountain Eagle and his stupid notions. "And no, it's not all good, it's just not all good, it's not, it's not!"

Which was when the hippie smile faded from Mountain's face as he felt Robert shaking hard under his kneading hands as if he were sobbing. The boy laid his chin on the older man's shoulders, his voice barely a whisper, "Aw Bobby, it aint that bad, it's gonna be all right…and, man, Clover, she's freakin' out, and neither of us want her losin' it. I know you know what I mean, Bobby, so let's just chill for today, I'll make some tea, we'll sit out here for a while, then go put on our suits and head on down to the beach."

Robert turned then, tears on his face. Clover ran over, pushed Eagle aside, wrapping her arms around Robert's shoulders. She put her head down and sobbed on his chest, his hands limp at his sides, tears skittering down his unshaven cheeks until he caught sight of Mountain Eagle's encouraging nods and lifted his good arm to embrace the girl, patting her on the back.

When they both had calmed down, Robert held her close and apologized for crying. He assured Clover in a whisper that he just needed a few days off—that he was just excited and a little on edge with Beryl coming that afternoon—and they could resume the exercises after she went back to Asheville.

Which was not what he intended to say at all. Not at all. But with her cowering in his arms, Clover was probably the only one left in the world that he could lie to.

And all that said, Robert Tevis knew in his troubled heart that, having once said those very words, that would be exactly what he would do...after Beryl came and went. And then Jen would arrive.

Chapter Twenty-Two

And so it went, day after day, Jed toiling in the fields of the Lord's servant; Marion tending to her stricken ex-husband, who was now living a few hundred yards away through the jungle with Mountain Eagle and Clover taking turns fending off his despair; Alyssa and Sam back in Elting in a tenuous dance with their families, each one privately atoning for their sins realized, sins misunderstood, sins uncommitted; Beryl traveling down to Manuel Antonio after completing multi-media lectures about animal behavior for college sophomores and juniors who had no visceral connection to their own animal natures; and then there was Jen Magruder, Robert's redemptive love, sitting alone in a gin joint in Oaxaca, wondering once again what the hell she had gotten herself into.

Mountain Eagle, Clover and Robert were still at the beach when Beryl showed up at Marion's home, sweaty and tired, already annoyed at everyone. She was two hours early.

Robert had grown to love the calm light blue waters in the cove, loved floating on his back, loved tilting his head back far enough for the water to fill his ears, bringing him all the way back to the Elting of his youth, hiking up to Split Rock, lying on his back just beyond the pounding waterfall, the cold water reverberating in his ears…and now it was the only place, the only place, beyond those occasional dreams of flying, where left arm and leg didn't feel quite so heavy, quite so lifeless.

Even though his strength and range of motion, especially in

the leg, had improved, Robert understood his bones and muscles would never return to the way they were before the strokes. "I'm goddamn sixty," he'd said to Marion and Leslie a few nights before during their once a week dinner, Mountain Eagle and Clover having left for a concert up in Jaco. "And I'm just now coming to realize that there's just no more Comeback Kid left in me. That's what they used to call me, y'know."

Leslie sighed, "Oh, Robert…" She reached over to pat his knee. "I'm so sorry. I can't imagine how difficult it must be, but if once you were a Comeback Kid maybe you could be one again now."

Which was when Marion sprayed the water in her mouth over the railing and gasped out a snorting laugh.

Leslie looked horrified. Robert red-faced.

"Robert, I'm sorry to laugh, but you were never the Comeback Kid, not in Chapel Hill, not in Elting…and certainly not here in Costa Rica, despite what that sweet girl Clover might be telling you. I mean, you're lots of things, Robert, but you are not now, not ever the Comeback Kid. Where in the hell did you come up with that?"

Refusing Marion's smiling face, he glanced sheepishly over at Leslie: "Sixth Grade—the Campus School."

Leslie laughed, slapping him on the thigh she had just patted. He looked over at Marion and couldn't tell whether she bit her lip to keep from laughing or crying.

That's what he was thinking about while floating on his back, arms outstretched, ears submerged—how Marion was right, and how she never allowed him his more heroic notions of himself—when Mountain Eagle appeared above him, a wild-haired apparition in the flawless blue sky, a broad toothy smile gurgling, "Bobby…Bobby…Bobby," and now that he caught his attention, reached down to grab his hand, pulling him up as Bobby dropped his better foot down on the silky sand and stood.

There was Beryl in a surprisingly modest floral skirted bathing suit wading through the knee-deep water, smiling so sweetly as she neared him, his SHIT necklace and the key dangling between her small breasts.

He couldn't contain his joy, reaching out for her with both arms and pulling her into his loving grasp, his face contorted with all the competing emotions of the last year. Over her shoulder he could see Clover and Mountain Eagle smiling so benevolently a few yards away. Or were they just laughing? Didn't matter, he tightened his grip on his baby girl. "I am so happy to see you."

"Hey Dad...I can't breathe," she said, her young face smushed into his hairy chest, "Let me look at you!"

Did he misstep? Lose his balance? So suddenly they were listing, Beryl wriggling to get out of his iron clinch, Robert holding on to her for dear life desperately trying to keep from toppling over onto his daughter.

And so with one great heave he flung himself backward into the warm Pacific, his arms clamped around Beryl's thin shoulders, his bushy head, then face slipping under the clear water's surface, Beryl twisting off his useless beached whale of a body.

Mountain Eagle was there in a flash, Robert's coughing horror turning into full-throated laughter as he was being pulled up, glancing then over at Beryl who wasn't laughing. "Just give me a few moments, baby girl, I'm, uh," righting himself and standing on his own, "I'm just uh—"

"What?" she said. She was on her knees, using her fingers as a rake to find the necklace that had ripped away when he grabbed her.

Robert took one step back, righted himself in the sand, and glanced down at the smooth white skin above his daughter's delicate eyebrows. "Hey, I'm sorry. I lost my balance. It's just so wonderful to see you, Beryl. I've been so looking forward to this—"

Beryl glanced over at Eagle and Clover. "He was squeezing the life out of me."

They shrugged. Smiles now plastered to their faces like they were high on peyote.

"I'm sorry, Beryl," Robert said again, stumbling now sideways through the water toward Clover and reaching out for her hand like one does a piling. "I'm sorry, sweetheart, I was just so glad—"

She held up the scavenged necklace and shook her head.

Robert turned away as if to walk to shore, but it was just a gesture. His leg was still to weak to go it alone.

Beryl stood there, hands on her thin hips, chest moving up and down, the sun behind her slipping under a puff of clouds. "I'm sorry I snapped at you, Dad—it was a long day, a hard day leaving Stephen behind. And," she paused, sunlit water glistening on her bare shoulders, "I guess I'm still working things out between the two of us. It's pretty complicated, you know."

He nodded. "I can help, though" he said, the old shrink's voice creeping in, and instantly wished he'd kept his tongue.

"Well, there we go again, Dad. That's the problem. You can't let go. So, my dear father, let's get this straight right now before it turns into something else: I am not your baby girl anymore. Get over it. I got out of that car a long time ago. If Alyssa wants that title, it's all hers. I'm grown up, a college professor. Just stop holding on so tight and give me some air."

Robert lifted his hands in surrender, one higher than the other. "No mas," he said with a grin. Then thinking all was well, he opened his arms for a hug.

"No mas," she said. And with that she lifted her chin, turned and started to splash her way out of the water muttering to herself about a sixty-year-old man saying "No mas."

Clover left Robert's side and ran through the churned up water after her. Robert watched helplessly as Clover put a sisterly hand on Beryl's shoulder, as Beryl gestured violently in the air, as she stepped so resolutely out onto the sand, swinging her long hair back over her shoulder.

Mountain laid a brotherly hand on Robert's shoulder. "Well, Bobby…women," he said with a smirk, "can't live with 'em, can't kill 'em."

Robert shook his head. "She needs a shrink," he said and coughed, laughing at his own joke. He turned dark then, "I'm never going to be able to get anywhere with that p-p-p-etulant child!"

Mountain had no idea what petulant meant, but he demurred, "I guess," adding a few seconds later as they sloshed up to the beach, "maybe she just had a bad day. I mean, that's a possibility, right?"

"No."

Now the young man and the old man watched the girls standing on the beach, Beryl still gesturing until she bent down and picked up something colorful off her towel. She turned around then, facing the blue water and the bluer sunset, facing her father, fidgeting with the broken clasp, the necklace dangling from her fingers—and slipped it over her head.

Robert had his eyes on his feet, glistening through the clear blue water. "See? That's what I mean! One moment she hates me and the next she loves me. I just don't get her."

Eagle's hand was quickly back on Robert's shoulder: "Looks like Clover has got everything under control, Bobby. Anyway, y'know, I really don't think she meant anything by it."

"You've got a lot to learn, my young friend. It may not seem so sometimes, but I did learn a few things along the way about human b-b-b-behavior." Then they were silent, standing shoulder to shoulder in thigh-deep water, neither knowing what to do next.

Beryl was shouting something from the beach. Then it was Clover calling through cupped hands, "We'll see you up at the cottage." The two women already heading for the trees.

Robert murmured, "Mountain…"

Mountain tilted his head like a golden retriever.

He spoke slowly, enunciating each word as Clover had coached him: "This is going to sound a little stupid, a little sappy after what just happened, b-b-but I don't think I ever thanked you and Clover enough for all you've done for me. Moments like this with my daughter remind me of what a jackass I've been. What a jackass I've always been. I don't think I'd have been able to survive without you and Clover."

Mountain was already shaking his head, "Aw, Bobby, dude… you'd a been fine without us, but we've been happy to go along for the ride—and besides, we're not done yet, right?"

Robert stood as still as the fronds on the palm trees, the small wake from a kayak lapping at his thick thighs.

"Right?"

"Right. The Dude abides."

"Whatever you say, Bobby."

"The Big Lebowski."

"Whatever you say, Bobby."

Robert, Clover, and Mountain Eagle were walking slowly and silently over to Marion's house, arriving just ten minutes past the invitation time. Robert, who had deliberately left his cane back at the cabin, stopped a few feet before the two back steps up to the small porch and turned to Clover. "So, what am I looking ahead to?"

"Oh, she's fine." Clover said. "She was still a little angry when I left her a couple of hours ago, but it really didn't have anything to do with you. She said something about her teaching gig and being away from Stephen." She climbed the three steps to the small back porch. "Anyway, I'm sure she's had a gin and tonic or something by now."

"I've got some stash," Mountain Eagle offered up, reaching into his pocket for the baggie he stuck in there before they left the cabin.

Robert shook his head no and then speaking to neither one in particular, "Y'know, Beryl was my b-b-buddy b-b-back in the day—went fishing with me, helped me mow the lawn, went to the dump with me on Saturdays—and then so suddenly she wasn't."

Mountain Eagle nodded his head unknowingly and said, "Cool!" But Clover just looked plain sad as she pressed her thin lips together, lifted her sunburned narrow shoulders and then let them drop.

"Well, let's go face the music," Robert murmured.

Mountain Eagle took Robert's arm just above the elbow, urging him up the steps.

On the deck, Robert stopped just short of the door. Eagle and Clover standing behind, no doubt figuring it would be better if they let him enter first. "I think I need another minute," he said, breathing forcefully in and out through his nose.

"Yeah yeah yeah, take all the time you need, Bobby." Eagle sat down on a white plastic chair, pulled a cigarette out from somewhere inside his ponytail and lit it. "That's cool, dude."

Robert was looking around the manicured backyard, the beautiful vegetable garden, the new trellis over by the shed, the new passion-flower vines winding their ways up to the top. "So, Bobby—" Clover started haltingly, "I hope I'm not intruding, but what happened with you and Beryl? I'm no psychiatrist like you, but it seems like she's pretty pissed at you."

Robert just shook his head. "I don't know. Nothing. A lot of things."

Clover shook her head, the beaded dreds clinking against each other, her vibrating breath exposing her nervousness.

"Clover," Mountain Eagle interrupted, "why don't you let the man be. He doesn't need two women giving him grief."

"I don't know," Robert repeated as if he didn't hear Mountain Eagle coming to his rescue.

"She's angry even when she's not angry, Bobby."

"Clover!" snapped Mountain Eagle.

She ignored him, too. "Something's not right, Bobby," she pressed on. "What happened? What did you do to her?"

Robert glanced up angrily. "What are you saying?"

"I'm not saying anything, just…" she scanned the yard again, tears blurring her vision. "I just know that sometimes—" She didn't finish.

Robert looked into her eyes, remembered in that instant what he knew about those kinds of looks from teenage girls and quickly swallowed the rising bile. He closed his eyes then and softened his voice: "Well, sweet girl, I promise that nothing like that ever, ever, ever happened between us. Ever."

"Well, what did happen?" she implored, a single tear rolling down her cheek and falling onto her peasant blouse.

"She was my pal."

Clover's lip was trembling. "And what?"

"And she grew up."

Clover shook her head, the strawberry dreds now shimmying like a bead curtain after someone walks through them.

He screwed up his face. "And things happened."

"Like what?"

"Clover!" Mountain hissed, a puff of smoke escaping his mouth.

She ignored him once again. "And what, Bobby? I need to know."

"And...and hmmm, I guess she thinks I didn't want her to grow up," his voice just above a raspy whisper, "and I couldn't let go."

The screen door swung open then with a rusty creak. "I thought I heard something."

It was Leslie, looking rather Hollywoodish in her platform wedge sandals, white Capri pants, a powder-blue, spaghetti-strap top, and one of her signature long toucan Scarves By Leslie. "What the hell are you three doing out here?" She looked over at Mountain Eagle. "You gladiators smokin' a big fat doobie before entering the Coliseum?"

Eagle held up the burning cigarette. "Just some American Spirit."

"Then come on in, y'all. No one's gonna bite you." She lowered her voice then, "Though I'd be careful whom you try to pet." She snickered at her own wit and held the door open. "Don't be shy."

Robert glanced over at Clover: "We'll talk some more when we get home. It's nothing bad. I've been a jackass, that's all."

Clover wiped a tear from her cheek, smiled weakly, and slipped her hand through his arm. Mountain Eagle squeezed out the burning ember from the cigarette, mashed it into 2 by 6 planks with his flip-flop until it was just a black smudge, and then tucked the cigarette back in his ponytail.

Holding the door open, Leslie extended her arm in welcome. "All right, gentlemen, please start your engines."

Chapter Twenty-Three

The small house smelled of the jungle, the casado on the stovetop along with fried plantains sizzling in butter. Robert could smell some kind of fish baking and a Russian salad was already prepared on the counter with beets, potatoes, hard-boiled eggs, and mayo.

Marion looked relieved, wide-eyed when the four of them walked out onto the veranda. She rushed up to kiss Clover hello, a quick breathless kiss on the cheek for Mountain Eagle, and finally a hug for Robert, pressing her lips against his ear and whispering, "Is everything okay?"

He had no words, just a quick nod.

On the long cocktail table were various small pocos, including patacones with black bean dip, chimichurri with tortilla chips, chifrijo with chicharrones, ceviche, and vigorón.

Beryl was in the yellow plastic Adirondack chair when they stepped through the doorway. Marion said, "Come say hello to our guests, Beryl."

Beryl smiled but didn't move. She reached over to the table for her tall gin and tonic, and rose.

It was then Leslie's turn to break through the purgatorial silence, "Come, come...take a load off," she said, gesturing to the couch and a rattan chair. "I'll bring out some drinks...Robert, I assume you'll have the usual Shirley Temple...and you two... guaro or Imperials?"

Marion turned then, "I'll get them," but Leslie reached across and grabbed her wrist, whispering, "Oh no, you're not leaving me out here with these hyenas. You sit down and I'll get the drinks." She winked at Clover, "And pour myself a little more guaro while I'm at it." ·

The five of them trained their eyes on Leslie as she deserted them on the veranda. Beryl put down her glass and, seconds later, picked it up again. Marion smiled over at Clover who, having felt never so ill at ease, smiled uneasily back at her. A few seconds later Mountain plucked the half-smoked cigarette out from his ponytail, put it in between his lips, breathed in through his nose, then took the butt out and placed it back in its "holder" in the back of his head.

Marion, slipping into her lifelong role as caretaker, reached for a tortilla chip and swept it through the chimichurri, handing it to Mountain. Then another for Clover, who held it up but didn't bring it to her mouth. Then one more for Beryl who shook her head twice, "No."

When she turned to offer it to Robert, he held up his hand, coughed, wiped his mouth with the back of his arm, and then pushed himself out of the rattan chair. He stood there, wobbly at first, and then, while all eyes were on him, Marion still holding the tortilla chip, walked slowly, deliberately across the cluttered veranda and over to Beryl, then extended his good hand, the swelling almost completely gone.

Beryl sat stone-faced for two-three-four-five seconds, then inhaled deeply and, ignoring his hand, pressed her hands down on the flat arms of the Adirondack chair and stood. Robert turned then and walked into the house, through the kitchen where Leslie looked up like a filly out in the meadow as he passed by and stepped out the back door with Beryl close behind.

"Should we take a walk?" he asked.

"Can you walk?"

"I can walk. Very slowly," he added with a sad smile, "and with a bit of a limp."

Beryl nodded and stepped down off the small deck onto the thick green grasses, walking over to the narrow road along the side of the house where she waited for her father.

"Do you want to see my little cabin?" he asked. "It's just a couple of hundred yards over that way." He pointed down two rutted lanes through the jungle, a monkey swinging through the branches above.

She shook her head. "Let's just walk," she said, scooting around him to his strong side and heading down toward the beach.

Robert imagined them both apologizing at the same time, like in all those romantic comedies that had punctuated his life since he was a child in Elting, cutting each other off two, three, four times, apologizing in unison each time, then laughing at the absurdity of it all…first one saying "You go first"; then the other saying "No, you go…."

They were nearing the main road when Robert's reverie came to an end; the two cinematic combatants should have been hugging, credits rolling, houselights going up, teary-eyed scattered applause.

"Beryl, I'm sorry," he spoke finally as they stopped on the raised sidewalk, his strong hand on her shoulder. "If that's what you're w-w-w-aiting for, I am truly sorry for what happened today."

"I don't know what I'm waiting for, Dad." Her voice was phlegmy, thick with the tears that were not flowing down her cheeks. "But no, I'm definitely not waiting for you to apologize. In fact, I'm going to apologize to you for acting like a brat before." Robert raised his eyebrows in surprise. "But you know as well as I do that it had nothing to do with the damn necklace."

She paused then, expecting some sort of reaction from him, but when there was nothing, she scowled and walked across the road.

When he caught up with her and reached out for her elbow, she turned. "What?"

With a deep sigh, he squashed the sudden desire to send the brat to her room, the insolent little child: "I just want you to tell me what I need to apologize for, Beryl. Tell me and I'll apologize."

She looked at him like he was from outer space.

"I know," he said, swallowing some bile for the second time in a day. "I know. I know. It's just that I've just been through hell and back and frankly I've come around to thinking I don't know anything anymore." He sat down on a bench. Beryl stood off to the side. "I know I have a lot of apologizing to do, Beryl, but I don't know where to start." He looked her straight in the eye and held her there for several seconds, something he hadn't done in a long long time, maybe going all the way back to when he would change her diapers, holding her tiny feet in one hand, three fingers, all the while cooing, talking so sweetly to his baby girl like he never talked to anyone ever before. Ever before. Their love child.

"This morning," he began, "I thought about the time I was late picking you up at kindergarten...do you remember that?" She raised her eyelids but didn't say anything. "Well, I was remembering seeing you all the way down at the end of the hall with your teacher, then how you were running my way with a big grin on your face and leaping into my arms...and then you were suddenly bawling and banging your fists on my chest, and I held your fists in my hand and told you never to hit me again."

She tilted her head. "I don't remember that."

"It doesn't matter, I guess. I'm just sorry for being such a jackass. I should've understood. The sorry truth is that I only did that because the teacher was watching and I didn't want her to think I was one of those "anything goes" psychologists."

She didn't speak then. But she sat down next to him on the bench and stared out at the water.

"And I'm sorry about the time I wouldn't let you go up the pyramid at Chichen Itza with your brother and sister. I'm sorry I sent you to your room that Christmas Eve when you threw the ornament at Alyssa." He paused then, a smirk followed by a hitch in his throat. "And I'm sorry I didn't protect you from Sam and Alyssa. I knew how they treated you, how mean they were to you. I am so sorry for so many things, Beryl…should I go on? If nothing else, I've had a lot of time to think about my failures as a father."

She closed her eyes then and slowly opened them, waiting for him to meet hers. "You really are a jackass, Dad. You think my anger is about you being a disappointing father?"

He winced. "I don't know."

"Well, it's just simply amazing that you have a license to practice psychotherapy."

He laughed, a long ago smoker's laugh. "I've come around to thinking that myself. And you're not the first one who's pointed that out."

He thought she'd laugh as well. She didn't.

Beryl was still staring out at the horizon. "I mean, what father in the history of the world didn't disappoint his kids?" Her voice grew softer. "Y'know, I've only been teaching a little while, granted, but I've already seen that it's only the really damaged ones who think their fathers did no wrong. I mean, fuck," Robert winced, "you should hear what I hear about abusive fathers driving their kids to ruin…and being praised for it." Now she was smiling. "Or speak to Clover some time like she isn't some kind of idiot. She'll tell you some hair-raising stories. And you were head and shoulders above that shithead Abraham…bringing his kid up to be slaughtered."

"So?"

"So what?" The edge was back.

"So why are you so damn angry at me?" His lips were trembling now. "Why do you hate me? Is it just because I cheated on your mother?"

Beryl bent her head and closed her eyes against the wrong storm welling up in her. When she beat it back, she raised her eyes and waited until Robert looked her way. "No...although what you did was really awful. It was vile and shameful, and it took me a long long time to get over it. I thought you were different." He was stone-faced. "But no, that's not it at all."

"So tell me." He took a deep breath. "Please."

"Well," she said and paused so long he thought she might never come out with it. "Well, to tell you the truth, it's mostly because you're such a self-righteous asshole you let Mom go without a fight. Because you were too good to go punch that snarky preacher in the nose. Because you betrayed all of us by being so goddamn disconnected from all those feelings you always tell everyone else they need to express."

Robert blanched. He had never once considered that he could have—or should have—tried to win back Marion. Especially after she took up with the damn pastor. "But she—"

Beryl stood up and pivoted, now looking down on the top of his head. "You didn't even fuckin' try."

She started to walk off, but turned, threw her hands up in the air, and sat back down on the bench. "Just like you didn't show up in Asheville. I kept waiting for you to knock on the door."

"I called...I called every day."

"Yeah, you called. You called. I know I said all that about water under the bridge, Dad, but you didn't knock on the damn door. You're the father. And you were the goddamn husband. And you didn't show up. You didn't punch that asshole preacher in the nose. You didn't come to my door."

This was not how Robert envisioned any of this supposed

reconciliation. He wanted to counter her, wanted to explain how it all happened with her, how he was only trying to do the right thing, how hurt he was, and the rage he felt when Marion told him about the pastor, but he was speechless, his whole body trembling, his tongue twisted like it was in the hours after the stroke left him lying flat on his back, strapped down on the gurney, looking up at the ceiling of the ambulance, the siren now piercing with the inescapable truth of her words.

"I don't know what to say," he said finally, reaching over with his weak hand and laying it on his daughter's knee. When she didn't cover his hand with hers or speak, Robert looked the other way and saw an apparition walking his way through the orange and red dusk on the beach. The apparition stopped twenty yards away and stared at the two of them. The man looked startled, wide-eyed, tanned face emptied of blood, his feet rooted into the sand.

By then Robert was gripping Beryl's knee with all his might, but there wasn't much might there. "Oh man, this is good, this is very good," Beryl said, perking up. "A little harmonic convergence, I'd say, a little karma, what goes around comes around, what's good for the goose." Her voice rose, "Hey there Jed!" she called across the beach.

"I really don't want to talk to him," Robert pleaded.

"Too late," she said. "The man's just as full of himself as you are. He's quaking in his goddamn Jesus sandals but he can't walk away."

She was right. Jed Blackstone was walking up the beach toward them like he might have imagined a man would walk carrying a cross. When he got to the bench, he clasped his hands below his belt and bowed his head. "Robert," he said, nodding. Then "Beryl."

"Hey there, Jed," Beryl broke through. "Fancy meeting you

here on this beautiful beach."

He didn't know how to respond, glancing over at Robert, whose elbows were on his knees, and whose eyes were on his own feet, not on the pastor. "How are you feeling, Robert?"

Robert didn't speak, a faint shake of the head.

"I-I don't know what to say," Jed went on, his voice fading in the gently lapping surf.

Beryl stood then. "Well, that makes two of you. Maybe you two can start by apologizing to each other for all the wrong reasons." Her eyes were sparkling with joy and pain.

"I was just telling my father that he should have punched you in the nose back when it would have meant something."

Jed chewed at his upper lip and glanced down at Robert, who sat stone-faced while Beryl strode off the beach, one, two, three, four steps, kicking up sand behind her.

Jed remained motionless, still holding his breath, as Robert pushed himself up off the bench with an unintended groan and limped off without a word. He saw that Beryl had stopped at the edge of the road, but had not turned around, her shoulders moving up and down, as if she was waiting for her father to catch up to her.

They walked slowly across the main road, the fatherly hand still on his daughter's shoulder, slowly, haltingly making their way up toward Marion's place when Robert finally spoke again. "You have to know that I am sorry, sweetheart—for all of it. If I had known—" He didn't finish.

"I know you are," she replied out of order, "but that doesn't make it all right. Besides," she was already smiling, "if a cow had balls…right?"

He smirked at his old friend Garrison's signature line. "But I want to make it up to you, Beryl. I will make it up to you…if it takes the rest of my life."

"Don't," she said. "You still don't get it, Dad. Just let it go. It's done and there's nothing to be made up. Things are just different now. I'll survive. We'll survive. And I'm done holding you accountable."

They turned off the narrow road into Marion's yard. Beryl got in front of Robert then and put her soft hand up to his face, just like her mother had done thousands of times. "You can't make it up to me, Dad. I love you, but you can't change what happened."

He nodded, not because he understood or agreed, but because agreement was all he had left in him. He remembered Siddhartha's advice to his friend Govinda, "Everything only needs my agreement, my assent...."

She stood up on her tiptoes and kissed him on the cheek.

When Beryl walked into the house without her father, the others were standing around the granite-top island separating the kitchen from the living room. They glanced back and forth among each other, then all at once the whole group was looking at her, waiting.

She shook her head in amusement. "He's coming," she said, "Jesus is coming," and walked out to the veranda to reclaim her drink, the ice cubes now melted, the glass wet on her fingers. She was trying to remember the whole Huxley quote about remorse to share with her father later, but could only come up with the last line: "Rolling in the muck is not the best way of getting clean."

Robert was just coming through the back door when Beryl returned to the living room. All motion paused in the room, the fading light flickering through the bamboo blinds. Everyone silent.

Robert stood in the doorway, leaned against the jamb and glanced around the room, glancing intently, one by one, into each set of eyes.

"Well, I'm starving," Leslie finally said when the wave got to her. She looked around, shattering the reverie: "The fish is overcooked, the plantains look a tad crispy, the salad is wilted, and I'm not getting any younger, so let's just slap on the ol' feedbag and get this party rolling."

Beryl, who surprised even herself, went over to Leslie and gave her a hug. "Yeah, who wants to make me a stiff drink that's not hot?"

"Me too!" Marion called out from the kitchen.

Mountain Eagle raised his hand a little too enthusiastically and, just for a moment, everyone laughed.

And thus with a margarita quickly down her gullet, Marion regained her color and her composure. Beryl was as merry as anyone had seen her since she was Drum Major in the marching band at Elting High. Even Clover seemed, at least momentarily, to let go of her own dismal story, the one she saw in everything she did.

So they ate and they drank and they drank some more and then drank some more and nothing was ever said about what had happened between Robert and Beryl down at the beach. Everyone laughed at how much of Robert's third margarita dribbled down his chin, how Mountain Eagle slurred his words, at Clover who passed out on the veranda. And neither Robert nor Beryl ever mentioned seeing Jed Blackstone.

And so Marion and Leslie, Mountain Eagle and Clover, each in their separate beds, went to sleep that evening assuming that father and daughter had had the cinematic moment Robert had imagined and made amends, hugged and kissed, shared a laugh at how stupid they were, and everything was back to the way it should be.

The way it never is.

Chapter Twenty-Four

Early the next morning Robert opened his eyes, looked up at the whirring ceiling fan, a cool wind on his damp forehead, the room suddenly spiraling. Swirling.

He clamped his eyelids shut then and soon felt the spinning blades—or was it the room itself?—slowing down, everything turning slower and slower and slower until it had slowed to barely a warm spring breath and then stopped, the sun on his face, the smell of lilacs in the still air.

Robert opened his eyes again feeling better than he had in months...since those easy days before the second stroke, when his life consisted mostly of wandering around beautiful and earthy Oaxaca, cheating on his diet and daily fantasizing about the luscious naked woman who shared his queen-size camper bed and who made him feel vital again.

He looked up at the whitewashed ceiling, held up his arms, and wiggled his fingers, then sliding his legs off the mattress almost effortlessly, and standing up without pain or stiffness, he stretched, and practically floated out of the tiny bedroom into the living room where sweet Clover was doing her morning meditations.

At the stove, Mountain Eagle was cooking oatmeal and raisins. Wearing only the white cotton drawstring pajamas Jen Magruder had bought for him in Mexico City, Robert reached both arms toward the ceiling, and then clenched his right hand, then his left, when he realized with some great satisfaction that there were no pins and needles in his fingers. Plus his fist suddenly seemed more of a rock than a beanbag. He did it again. "Something's happened," he said out loud. "Something's happened!"

Mountain Eagle turned his head like his avian namesake and surveyed the scene with a dreamy smile, still stirring the oatmeal. But Clover jumped up out of her meditation, those dark eyes wide open, palms up as if she was holding back a mud slide, "What? What happened? Are you okay Bobby? What's happening? Oh my God, Bobby!"

Robert swallowed the haughty fatherly laugh that, after all this time, came all too naturally from his lungs, suddenly and unaccountably brimming with gratitude and love for those he now called his adopted children, his beautiful young saviors, and promptly danced out the door onto the porch. A beautiful green iguana scampered across the lawn as the man stood and surveyed his paradise. At this moment, Robert felt so full of the utter vibrancy of life that he practically skipped down the three steps to the thick lawn, softer on his bare feet than he ever remembered it being, laying down on his back, the dewy grass tickling his bare skin, the sea a million stars.

As he lay there staring up into the endlessly blue firmament, Robert held up his hands again, balled them into tight fists, *hard as the Shawangunk conglomerate*, he thought and smiled, then lifting his arms up to the bluer than blue sky in exultation, in prayer, in devotion, beams of bright yellow light extending from his fingertips, feeding the sun.

And in that rarest of rare moments in a lifetime of such exceedingly rare moments of peace and joy, Robert Clemens Tevis felt so healthy, so blissful, so free of what his former friend and cuckold Garrison often called the "onerous disease of life," he closed his eyes against the light and saw all those stroke-inducing clots in his brain dissolving, breaking away and flowing down through his neck like a sparkling waterfall, moving across his shoulders and up his outstretched arms and fingers, floating up and out into the vast, vast, vast, vast, vast, sparklingly vast cosmos like children's bubbles.

After a while he heard (or thought he heard) beautiful, lovely, loving Clover calling him from the cottage, but there was no time now to dally, no time to eat the mush Mountain Eagle so devotedly prepared for him, no time even to dress. He had to see Beryl, her alabaster skin, the mournful look in her green eyes; he had to see Marion, those other-worldly blue eyes, her soft hand on his cheek.

He had to see Marion.

He rolled over and pushed himself up off the ground, walking, then striding down the sandy path to the unpaved road, his white cotton pajama bottoms riffling in the warm morning air, Clover's plaintive call in the breezy background, now just a bee buzzing, striding across Marion's newly mowed lawn to the redwood deck behind the house, opening the screen door.

Robert knocked three times on the Dutch door, but let himself in before anyone appeared. There was Beryl in the messy kitchen wearing an oversized pink T-shirt, pouring herself some coffee. She didn't turn around. "I love you with all my heart," he said.

She didn't seem to hear him. She slid the pot back into the coffeemaker and scooped some sugar into the cup.

"I need to see your mother first, though," he said, walking behind her, "but I'll see you in a minute." There was no reply.

Beryl brought the cup to her lips with both hands. Although she did not turn around, he thought she must have smiled. Moving out of the kitchen, he thought she must have looked amused.

Standing then in front of the louvered bedroom door, Robert brushed off the blades of grass still stuck to his shoulder blades before turning the brass knob and slipping inside.

Marion didn't wake up as he padded across the seagrass rug to the bed, and she didn't wake when he stood over her, chest heaving, pulse racing as he pulled the drawstring on his pajamas, the white cotton cascading down his legs.

She didn't wake or even stir as he lifted the cotton blanket and slid in next to her; didn't move as he placed his trembling hand around her naked back and pulled himself close, fingertips sliding down into the small of her back, now seeking out the scar on her hip, now caressing her soft bottom, his dry lips pressed to hers when she turned over, his breath passing into hers, her breathing slow and steady, slow and steady.

Chapter Twenty-Five

Pastor Henriquez found Jed sitting on the steps of the parsonage after he returned from his usual Monday afternoon visits to the shut-ins. "Brother Blackstone, you are just the man I want to see."

Jed, who had seen the Pastor drive up in the rusted old Impala, squinted up into the low sun and, for no reason he could figure, pretended to be surprised to see him. "More chores?"

Henriquez laughed, more a high-pitched giggle than Jed ever thought appropriate for a man of the cloth: "No, no, no, no, no ," he said, and then waited a few seconds until he could see that Jed was on the edge of some muttering annoyance. He sat down next to the younger man. "No, Brother Blackstone, it turns out that I need to be out of town this Sunday coming—called to service in San Jose—and I was hoping that you would conduct the service for me here. Si?" He sat down on the newly painted steps with a muffled "oomph."

"No." Jed shook his head.

"No?"

He turned to look at the older man. "I'm very sorry, Pastor Henriquez. It turns out that I won't be able to do that for you. In fact, I've just been sitting here, waiting for you to come back so I could say good-bye," said Jed," and then a few tremulous moments later, "and, of course, to say thank you for everything you've done for me." He thought to stand but stayed where he was.

The Pastor stood, reached for a Newport cigarette in his breast pocket, slipped it between his lips, and lit it. "I require no thanks, son. I do what I do to serve the Lord. That's all."

Jed grimaced. He looked up at the short man like he was about to say something, but his lips did not move.

The pastor sucked in deeply on the cigarette. "I am curious, though, about where you're going," he said, several seconds after the smoky exhale, "and why you think it will be different from here." He smiled, not unkindly, trails of smoke still escaping his lips.

Jed stood up then, ran his long fingers through his curly hair, his weary eyes pooling, "I have much work to do to cleanse my soul. I have to make things right. So I've decided that I'll be leaving tomorrow. I've done all I can do here. I'm sorry I can't—"

The Pastor reached up and patted the acolyte's shoulder. "What is it that the baseball player says? It's not done until it's done?"

Jed smiled. "Close enough. But I am done, Pastor Henriquez, it's done. I have miles to go before I sleep."

The Pastor raised his thick eyebrows and then lowered himself back down on the steps.

Jed followed the Pastor's lead and sat down again beside him, leaning over and snagging a thick blade of grass, sticking it between his teeth. "Sorry. That's a line from a poem by Robert Frost." And when he saw no nod of recognition from the little man at his side, he added, "'Stopping By the Woods on a Snowy Night,' it's called."

Henriquez shrugged, pushed his palm down on Jed's knee and stood back up. "So tell me Brother Blackstone, where are you going, what will you do? What are you leaving behind? Who will have you?"

Jed lowered his head. "I am going back to New York, to Elting. Back to my church…to face the music. I can't run away my whole life."

"Music? Is that what you call penance back in the States?"

He looked up squinting, smiled boyishly. "I guess."

The old pastor placed his thick leathery palm on the man's head. "Well, my friend, I wonder if maybe they just see Jesus in America, but not the cross. You can't separate them, Brother Blackstone, and there is no music on the cross, just the cry of humanity. Si?"

Jed's face darkened. "No."

"No?"

There followed a long exhalation. "It's a different world up there," said Jed.

"Different? How can it be different?"

Jed shook his head again. "I'm not sure I can explain it to you."

Now the Pastor stepped one pace to the left and blocked the sun. "Oh, I think I understand, Brother Blackstone. I understand. But I must admit that I don't understand the urgency of your departure, why there's no way you can stay around here for just four more days? Are you running away from something down here? Do you have to get back there immediately to turn on the Victrola? Put the needle on the record yourself? And it has to be tomorrow, Pastor Blackstone? It cannot wait until Monday?"

Jed angled his jaw and glared into the old man's dark bloodied eyes, but said nothing.

"After all this time you can't find it in your heart to do the congregation this one simple favor?"

Jed shrugged. "I'm sorry, I just…I made up my mind last night and I'm afraid…" pressing his lips together, "if I don't leave right now I'll never again have the strength to face up to my failings."

"That sounds like an excuse I hear from the boys in the youth group: 'Oh my mama needs me,' 'I have a stomach ache,' 'I think I'm coming down with something,' 'I'm afraid….'"

"But it's true." Tears were now rolling down Jed Blackstone's unshaven cheeks. "If I don't leave now I'm not sure what will happen to me."

The Pastor stepped up onto the newly painted porch and wiped his hands on the back of his pants. "Well, Jed Blackstone, you have a good heart, I know that. But if you leave me now all weepy and pathetic, I guarantee you'll walk the desert all your days." He opened the screen door to the chapel, walked inside the cool, dark sanctuary, and sat down in the first row of pews.

Jed Blackstone bent his head. He sat there on the porch for a long time, an eternity it seemed, before getting up, and following the old man into the sanctuary.

Alyssa was beside herself, hands on her hips, smudged mascara around her dark eyes. "I don't believe it!"

She looked around the room, scanning the bloodless faces of her husband Barry, her children, her brother, her sister, glaring now at her mother who leaned bleary eyed into her friend Leslie's shoulder: "I tell you this, Mother: That mother fucking priest is not going to bury my father!"

No one said a word until Leslie said very calmly, "He's not burying your father, Alyssa, he's just—" cut off instantly by Alyssa jabbing her finger through the air.

Marion looked out from bloodshot eyes. "You have to know I'm as dismayed as you are, Alyssa—maybe more so—but Pastor Henriquez is up in San Jose and he asked and—"

"And I don't give a flying fuck where he is. That sonofabitch is not going to say a single solitary word about my father!"

Barry, still in his traveling clothes after the twelve-hour journey from Elting, quickly ushered the children into the kitchen with Clover and Mountain Eagle. When he returned to the deck, he put his arm around his distraught wife. "Hey there," he said softly, "let's try to figure something out." Then pressing his lips against her ear, whispered, "You're goddamn scaring the kids."

"To hell with the kids!" she muttered, a waterfall of tears flowing down her red cheeks. And then in a whisper, "And fuck you, Barry, you're not going to make this all better. You're not going to silence me. We're not back in Elting anymore." She picked up a glass off the rattan table and threw it into the jungle. "I have to get out of here," she said, turning and walking off the lanai into the living room and out the back door, the screen slapping against the frame.

Leslie held Marion's wet cheeks between her fingers and looked straight into her eyes. Then gave her a peck on the cheek and turned, clearing the glasses off the coffee table, picking up a crumpled napkin from the rug, and walked back into the house. Barry, Sam, Beryl, and Marion following in silent procession, each sitting down on the couch and the end chairs like scolded children.

"It's hard," red-eyed Mountain Eagle offered from behind the messy kitchen counter.

Beryl opened her mouth to say something but kept it to herself, waving her hand back and forth. Sam put his arm around his sister.

"I'm going to take the kids out into the backyard," Clover said, already picking up Haley and grabbing Travis's hand. Mountain Eagle followed them out of the house, and when the ones left behind heard the slap of the screen door, Sam asked, "What are we going to do about them?"

Marion pointed out the door. "You mean Mountain Eagle? Clover? We're not going to do anything, Sam. They're just some sweet kids who loved your dad." She looked at Beryl who was nodding. "They're just kids who somehow found a way to let the man express his love without making it feel like a noose. I suspect they'll just move along after all is said and done. And I, for one, am very sorry about that."

Sam turned, eyebrows arched, looking over to Barry for some support, but Barry held up his hands in surrender: "I've already been told to keep my distance." He smiled. "And you know your sister."

Leslie walked back into the circle, drying her hands on a dishtowel, then sat down on the arm of the couch next to Marion. She touched her friend's shoulder. "Well, let me take care of some organizing."

No one said a word.

"Well...o-kay. So tell me Sam, when will Glenda and Aaron be arriving?"

Sam's voice was full of phlegm. "The plane arrives in San Jose at two-thirty, so...five-thirty?"

Leslie nodded. "Six-thirty...seven... All right, that's a start. Marion? You said Robert's friend Garrison is coming?"

Marion, who was then staring down at a tiny green bug in the grass rug, would not lift her head. "I don't know," she whispered. "I don't think Robert would want him here."

Sam opened his eyes wide but didn't say anything. Marion continued as if nothing had happened, "He just emailed me this morning and said that he was going to try to fly down. But he's got to find someone to take care of his wife."

"Yes, yes," Leslie said, as if putting check marks next to a list. "So now there's that Jen Magruder person." She reached over and squeezed Marion's shoulder. "I'm sorry, but—"

Marion shook her head, said something so low no one heard.

"Well," said Leslie, "did someone say that Clover had contacted Ms. Magruder?"

Again silence.

Leslie waited a few seconds, then said, "I guess it doesn't matter. There's nothing we have to do, right?" Nothing. She stood up. "So I guess that's it," looking around the room at the somber group, "but, oh no! I forgot about Stephen. When's the tall drink of water coming down?" a wry smile crinkling up the corners of her eyes.

Beryl held out her palms, more tears falling off her cheeks onto the peasant blouse. "I killed him," she moaned. "I killed him."

Dressed in the wrinkled robe he had angrily stuffed in a suitcase before leaving Elting, Jed Blackstone stood alone on the newly painted front steps of the small, simple chapel in Manuel Antonio. Beyond the open doors in the empty sanctuary were eighteen sanded, stained, polyurethaned benches, a prayer book on each place where a parishoner might sit, and at the front, leaning on the altar, an 18 by 24 charcoal portrait of Robert Tevis done by Clover, touchingly unschooled. And in front of that, raised up on flat stones, a simple urn.

Pastor Blackstone pushed up his sleeve and looked at his watch—9:17. The service was to begin at 9:30. He turned and walked back into the sanctuary, up the aisle, pausing at each row to check that there were prayer books for everyone, and then stood at the altar, clasping his hands behind his back, then in front. And after he glanced up at the cross, Jed Blackstone closed his eyes

"Heavenly Father, I come to you now," he said. "Lord, I am a sinner. I have sinned against you, even this day, but Lord, I come and humbly ask you in the name of your Son, Jesus Christ, that you will forgive me for my sins, that you will wash me in the blood of my Savior and I shall be cleansed. I beseech you and thank you now for saving me. Come into my heart and into my life and Lord, lead me by your Spirit and help me to live for you from this day forth. I thank you now in Jesus' name."

Footsteps interrupted his prayer, and he whispered a quick

"Amen" before turning to the intruder, a thin woman in black, framed in the white light of the double doorway. He couldn't make out her face.

Pastor Blackstone cleared his throat. "Are you here...here for the Robert Tevis service?"

"Yes," she said, not moving, still in the doorway. "Is there a problem? Has it been canceled?"

He moved one step, two steps down the aisle, and stopped. "Not that I know of, but I am, well, you know, aware that the family has had some concerns," he paused, "about how the service should go and I am, hmmm, I have not been privy to all the various discussions."

Jen Magruder turned then and saw two somber women in black walking up the stone path with a tall boy, his hair pulled back in a long ponytail, and a thin little waif of a golden-haired girl with dreds. The boy was wearing a white shirt a size or two small for his long arms, black slacks a size or two too large, and sandals. The barefoot girl wore a gaily colored patchwork dress. Both were smiling incongruously, beatifically.

The group of four paused at the steps and looked up at Jen Magruder. Jen smiled weakly and, looking at Leslie, "Marion?"

Leslie shook her head with a smirk and tilted her head toward Marion.

"Oh! I'm sorry...leave it up to me to have a fifty-fifty chance of getting it wrong, right?"

"You must be Jennifer," said Leslie.

"Jen." She dropped her canvas purse and walked across the porch and down the steps, her hand extended toward the bereft Marion. "I'm so very sorry."

Marion took her hand. "Nothing to be sorry about, Jen, you couldn't have known what I look like, right?"

"No, right. I meant that I'm so sorry about Bob."

She lowered her eyes. "Me too."

"Thank you," Jennifer said, not sure whether that was the right response.

Then there was nothing more to say. The air was still, soon to be hot. Behind Jen Magruder there was Jed Blackstone standing rigid, silently filling the doorway in his wrinkled black robe.

"I'm Leslie, a friend of Marion's—and more recently Robert's. And these are Robert's friends Mountain Eagle and Clover, who I think you know. Best as I can tell, the two of them just ate some peyote."

Jen smiled. "Yes, these two I know all too well," she said, striding over and extending her arms to give them a singular hug, high and low. Mountain Eagle rested his cheek on Jen's head. Clover leaned into her breast.

Jed Blackstone cleared his throat and said, "Hello, Marion."

"Jed!" she said as if she just noticed him. "I-I...," she laughed nervously, "I really don't know what to say. This has got to be the weirdest moment of my entire life."

His eyes were wide open and his forehead deeply wrinkled. "Ranks right up there for me as well."

"I mean," she said turning to Leslie, "here I am at my husband's funeral with my husband's girlfriend and my ex-lover and—thank God for you, Leslie, especially for not having slept with anyone in this bizarre crew—or did I speak too quickly?"

Leslie put her arm around her friend's shoulder. "Not yet, dearie," she said and waited the requisite three beats, before adding, "just kidding."

This, the fourth or fifth awkward silence, was broken by Clover, arms up in the air and crying out to the heavens, "Oh Bobby, my Bobby! This is so beautiful, all of us who love and adore you, here together in this holy spot, here to wish you good passage on that stairway to heaven."

And just as Clover's air ran out, Mountain Eagle picked it up, "Amen! Amen! Amen! And what can I say but far, far, far-out, Bobby, you are the farthest-out man I ever knew and yes, it's a far, far, far better thing you do now than anyone has ever done anywhere in the universe." He lifted his fist in the air and screamed, "You are the man, Bobby Bob!"

"Oh my," Jen Magruder laughed, "I guess they did eat some peyote." She took each of them by the hand and gently led them off the pebbled path and around the back of the small church.

Pastor Blackstone was not so amused by the outburst. "Perhaps someone should keep those two outside."

Marion scowled. "They're just kids, Jed, and they don't know what to do with their grief." She turned then and whispered to Leslie, "I hate to say it, but I'm glad that Sam and Alyssa weren't here to witness that."

Looking properly chastised, his hands clasped in front of his robes, Jed pressed his lips together and asked Leslie, "Will the others be following?"

"No, Jed," Marion answered before Leslie had an opportunity to speak. "Unfortunately, they have refused to join us—and have arranged to carry Robert's remains back to Elting for a memorial service back home." Tempted to repeat Alyssa's condemnation of the pastor, something akin to better sense allowed her to hold her tongue.

"So this is it?" he pressed on.

"I'm afraid so," Leslie said.

"Dr. Fitzgerald won't be joining us?"

Marion's eyes were pooling now. "No, Garrison couldn't get away. He'll be joining the kids at the Elting ceremony. It's probably just as well."

And so Marion and Leslie walked into the chapel behind Pastor Blackstone, a slow and silent procession moving past the nine rows of newly stained and sanded benches, pausing at the simple urn and Clover's childish charcoal portrait of Robert behind the wheel of the RV.

Leslie left Marion's side then and walked around the altar to the back door. When she returned a minute or two later, she was followed by the two beatifically smiling hippies, Mountain Eagle with his index finger in front of his lips, and a somber, teary Jen Magruder, whose grief had replaced her momentary amusement at the situation.

When they were all seated in the first row, left side, Jed stepped up to the platform and stood stiffly behind the wooden lectern. He began with his planned remarks, welcoming everyone, acknowledging the strange and mysterious forces that had brought all of them together in this place, affirming that the Lord has a plan for all of us, that everyone should take comfort that He has welcomed Robert into the Kingdom of Heaven.

By the recitation of the 23rd Psalm, a verse that normally brought great comfort to Marion, she experienced no sense of comfort whatsoever.

Mountain Eagle sat transfixed by the cross above the back wall, an unwavering smile across his face. Clover was leaning on his shoulder, asleep. Marion saw the Pastor's eyes open wide and quickly turned to see Beryl, framed by the light in the door, and then slipping into the rear pew.

Jen got up with a breathy "I have to…," but Marion and Leslie didn't seem to notice, sitting there looking stoic and unbowed, holding hands. Marion was wondering about her other two children and whether they'd be there when she got back to the house.

When Jed seemed to finish—at least it seemed he was no longer speaking, just standing behind the lectern with a flat smile forced upon his face—Marion looked behind and saw Jen

Magruder sitting in the back row with Beryl.

After a few uncomfortable moments trying to find some whispered mutual expression of their loss, the unrelated guilt they each felt about his death, Jen and Beryl had begun talking about the man that linked them—how awful and wonderful he was, and how, if only Robert would have let himself, he might have pushed through the prison that psychology condemned him to. Jen pointed to the strange necklace that hung from Beryl's neck. "He told me about that."

That provoked a smile. "He was such a jackass." Which made them both a little sadder.

And when they looked up, Marion, her face flushed with tears, was standing over them with the urn in both hands. "I'm glad you came, Beryl."

"I didn't—"

"I know. I'm just glad you came." She pushed the urn forward. "I'm going to transfer half the ashes to another urn for Sam and Alyssa—and then I'm going to scatter these in the ocean. Will you join us?"

Beryl glanced behind her mother. Leslie was now standing between the eternally-smiling Clover and Mountain Eagle, ashes now smeared on their foreheads.

Marion could feel Jed Blackstone's eyes on them as the odd congregation of five souls moved down the pebbled path. Just as they reached the edge of the dirt road, he called out for Marion.

She turned and, squinting into the glistening waters of the Pacific Ocean, saw the black-robed man waving one white hand her way, the urn in the other. Leslie grabbed her hand and said, "Just ignore him, babe. There's nothing back there for you."

But Marion, still squinting, shook her hand loose and, saying

"I'll only be a minute," walked back up the gravel path. "I still have some words I need to speak to him."

———————————

Forty-five minutes later, Marion stepped out of the dark chapel into the blinding morning light, eyes blurry, a different urn clasped between her hands, She scanned the newly mowed lawn. There was no one around. She had expected to find the five of them sitting together in the grass; had assumed that Leslie was playing "camp counselor" again and getting everyone to share memories of Robert; later on instructing them to close their eyes and, holding hands in a circle, lead them on one of her guided visualizations to a beautiful glistening waterfall where they'd be sanctified in His presence.

She rubbed the bursts of light from her eyes with her forearm and scanned the unbroken expanse of lawn again. There was no one there, just one of those enormous green iguanas scooting into the brush.

"Looking for someone?" Leslie snickered. And when Marion turned to find her friend sitting cross-legged on the floor of the porch, leaning back on the white clapboard, she added, "Jen took them all home—the Mountain boy and the flower girl were beginning to crash."

Marion nodded vacantly. She held out the new urn, looking over Leslie's shoulder. "We split up the ashes."

"I don't think Beryl went with them. She stuck around for a few minutes and when I went behind a tree to pee she must have left."

"I don't want to go home. I don't think I can face the others right now."

Leslie put aside her own carefully choreographed plans for the time being. "Come to my place then."

"I'm just so sad…and angry. I'm so angry, Leslie, that I could have stabbed that half-a-man in there…and I don't know what I might say to Alyssa and Sam. I'm just so disappointed. In everyone. Even Robert. I mean, how could that asshole have left me with all this?"

Leslie put her arm around her friend's shoulder and led her down the steps, down the pebbled path, and over to the dirt road.

On the way over to her tiny caretaker's apartment behind Hotel La Colina, a few steps from the preserve, Marion told Leslie about how Jed wept and apologized for his failures and how he had hurt her. That he was returning to Elting. To repent. To face his accusers.

"I picked up a Bible and threw it at him." She glanced over at Leslie to see how bad that sounded.

Leslie shrugged, "Could've been worse."

It was already hot, a lazy Saturday, vendors setting up their tables along the potholed beach road, bleary-eyed surfers, boards under their brown arms, wandering down to the beach, Capuchin monkeys swinging through the rafters and snarling at the brunch crowd at oceanfront hotels.

Jen Magruder was back in Robert Tevis's small cottage with Mountain Eagle and Clover, both sleeping, spooning on the futon couch. She sat at the small kitchen table, occasionally sipping some lukewarm coffee, wondering again, as she had often wondered in Texas, then Oaxaca, then Mexico City, what spell that man had had on her. There was nothing she could think of that, in the past, would have moved her toward him. He certainly wasn't handsome or sexy or young enough. And he was definitely not a "father figure"—inadvertently she made air quotes in the humid air, then glancing over to Clover and

Mountain to make sure they weren't awake—as she was long past looking for her own deadbeat father to wrap his arm around her; long past believing that any man was going to save her; Marcel put an end to that...and her career in four-star kitchens. She let her mind wander all the way back to finding her young husband with a needle in his arm; how she was long past saving any man who couldn't save himself.

But there was something in Robert's hurt soul, something in his utter confusion, something in his sweet, embarrassed smile that she couldn't get out of her head. Then or now. Something that made her laugh. That po'boy sauce running down his chin the first time she met him. How he got lost on the streetcar. The way he was just figuring things out that he should have learned decades before. The way he drove the Winnebago, left elbow out the window, a brand new grin barely peeking through his lips at the world just whizzing by. The smell of his T-shirt when he hugged her.

Then, with nothing to do and nowhere to go, at least until the kids woke up, she wandered into Robert's tiny bedroom and started to tidy up; first stripping the bed, the smell of him consuming the warm air all around her; tossing the sheets, pillowcases, dirty clothes in the corner; rubbing her hands on the back of her slacks as if to wipe the memory of him off her flesh. Then she found the bedspread, folded neatly on a chair, shook it out and spread it over the bare mattress, pulling it straight, tossing the pillows neatly back against the headboard.

Next she took the stained and smelly bottom sheet and spread it out on the bare floor and looked around. The wastebasket was full of tissues, there were apple cores on the bedside table right beside the vials of medicine he would take 2, 3, 4 times a day, and here and there, under the bed and around the baseboard, crumpled pieces of spiral notebook paper. She picked one up and unfolded it, intending only to use it to grab the dried apple cores without having to touch them. But when she saw that he had begun to write something, Jen could not keep herself from what she considered invading his privacy. In wobbly script, she read, "Should I die before I speak to a lawyer, I hope you will all respect my wishes and do the following"—then there was no more writing, but he had scratched a single squiggly line through "before I speak to a lawyer," before crumpling up that piece of paper and throwing it on the floor.

She shivered, wadded it back up and threw it in the middle of the sheet. Then ignoring the ten or twelve other wads of paper scattered around the dusty floor, Jen Magruder turned to the wastebasket and shook out the nasty contents on top of the sheet. Next were the pill vials and then the balled-up top sheet and pillowcases. Then, without thinking or breathing or wasting a single movement, she started gathering up the remaining pieces of paper and one by one tossing them into the pile.

As she scooped up the last one, though, instead of tossing it on the pile, she made a fist around it and crushed it until her bicep ached...opening her fist and looking at the wadded paper like it was something vile and disgusting, something that would burn her tongue and then her esophagus if she gnashed it into her mouth, as she was tempted to do, and swallowed it.

She raised her upper lip and pulled the edges of the paper away from each other, smoothed it out and read:

"My dear children,

If I die before I get a chance to speak with you, I hope you will all respect my wishes and do the following"—on this one he had crossed out "respect my wishes."

She tossed it on the pile. Then opened the drawer on the bedside table and, without actually looking at what was in there, turned it over and dumped pens, scraps of paper, a thermometer, paper clips, coins, sticks of gum, a photograph of her in Mexico City, a baseball card, a picture postcard from Oaxaca, sliding down off the growing mound of garbage.

She was tempted to snatch up the photograph, but didn't want to touch it, didn't want to have to keep it with her for the rest of her life, so she found the four corners of the sheet and, leaning over the pile, drew them up and tied the opposite ends together, hauling it over her shoulder, the smell of him following her out of the bedroom, across the living room and out the door where she saw Beryl just about to climb the steps to the porch.

The two women stared at each other like wild animals stunned by the other's unexpected presence in the jungle—for the briefest sunlit moment connected in ways beyond territory, family, hunger, thirst, fear—the spell broken when the bedsheet sack slipped off Jen's shoulder and dropped to the porch floor. "Just doing a little cleaning," she said.

Beryl looked as stricken as she had back at the church. "Don't throw out anything that—"

"I won't," she said. "I wouldn't."

Beryl just stood there, arms at her side, when she spotted a thin spiral notebook sticking out from beneath the mattress.

She opened it, read the first page, turned the sheet and read the second. Then she handed it to Jen, who nodded, her lips quivering, more tears flowing down her lined cheeks.

Neither one moved. A still life, Beryl thought.

"Tea?" Jen said a few moments later. "Would you like some tea?"

Beryl stared out the window. "I don't think I can go back there right now. Everyone's so angry, rushing around furiously, on the phone, making reservations, all of them packing up."

"Come," Jen said, extending her hand. "I'll put on some water. I don't think I can do anything else now."

Beryl took her hand and the two walked into the kitchen.

" I was just about to go through his drawers and fold some of his clothes," the older woman said. "I'm sure someone in the family would want them."

"Don't bet on it."

Chapter Twenty-Six

With the trial finally over, the charges withdrawn, Sam Tevis and his sister Alyssa were sitting in Diesing's Bakery in Kingston, alone at the end of a rectangular table set for eight. He held up a cup of coffee to toast her "freedom," and Alyssa, holding the handle of her mug with pink fingers sticking out of a cast, barely kissed her cup against his. "What a long strange trip it's been, Sis."

She couldn't talk, the time for talking long past, pressing her lips out in that pouty way that used to rile their father. "Don't give me that look!" he'd say.

"So...where are they? I thought everyone was coming right over after the dismissal." He poured copious amounts of sugar into his cup, stirred and brought the cup to his lips.

Alyssa shrugged, still not able to talk.

Then looking back at the door, Sam put the cup down and whispered, "So...do you think Mom's a lesbian?"

That made her laugh. "No. Well, we've already been through this...and it's not that I haven't thought about it, but I don't think so." Her eyes brightened then, the silent grief disappearing in the fluorescence of the diner. "You know Mom, Sammy...I think she likes the old horizontal mambo much too much," laughing then at her own joke.

Not Sam. "Jesus Christ, Alyssa, that's just plain disgusting!"

She smirked, the Tevis smirk. "Sorry. I guess there's been no action for poor Alyssa since Barry walked out on her, if you get my drift."

He watched his sister's face crumbling across the table. "I'm so sorry, Al. This whole thing has been hard on all of us, I mean, Glenda and me, we—"

Just then the glass door swung open and Marion, Leslie, Glenda, Beryl, and Stephen came in with the blowing snow. Leslie pointed to the table and the five made their way through the lunchtime maze.

There was the usual bustling around, taking off coats and hats, sitting down, blowing on hands, remarking about how easy it is to forget how nasty winter can be, picking up the thick menus, the silence. Sam lifted his water glass, "To Alyssa," he said, "and to all's well that ends well."

"Amen!" said Marion, pushing her glass of water through the air as if to clink each of the raised waters around the table.

Beryl, three months pregnant and already round of face, wondered, "So…why do you think he finally decided to drop the charges?"

No one said a word, each one looking around the bright table as if this was a game show and one contestant held the secret to Alyssa's salvation. Finally, Leslie stood up and raised her glass again, "To Marion!"

Alyssa's jaw dropped. "Did you go see him?"

Marion was shaking her head vigorously. "No!" Then it was her turn to smirk. "Well, yes, I did go see him, but he didn't want to hear anything from me. And I mean nothing…so no, it wasn't me. I tried but—"

Sam tilted his head to the side like their old golden retriever Hildie. "But you must've said something; he must've heard something. Yes?"

"No. No, no, no, no, no … well, yes, I said a lot of things, but he wouldn't even look at me. You should have seen me…I followed him around the rectory like a stalker, but he just acted as if I wasn't there. That's it. So I left and—" She stopped then, her face dropping into immeasurable sadness.

Everyone's eyes were trained on her now, waiting. "There's nothing to tell," she said finally, "I told him what Alyssa told the police…she was distraught at her father's death, at all the terrible fighting in the family, at the fact that he of all people was going to lead the memorial service, yadda, yadda, yadda…and when she saw him sitting on the same plane, she just snapped."

"A right cross I think it was," Sam snickered. His wife elbowed him and told him to behave himself.

"I, for one, am sorry we missed it," said Beryl.

"It was not pretty," Alyssa said.

"I can still see the look on his face," Sam said, "the tooth flying out of his mouth!" He grinned and then howled at his own joke like some overgrown monkey, flying through the trees in Costa Rica.

Glenda looked disgusted. "Who are you? I mean, she broke his damn jaw, Sam."

After the waitress interrupted the scowling silence and took their orders, Sam collected all the menus and handed them to her across the table. Only then Beryl said, "So, I still don't get it, Mom. What happened? Why did he just drop the charges all of a sudden?"

Marion shrugged.

"Frankly, I don't know why you won't tell them," Leslie said.

Marion pressed her lips together. It seemed for a moment as if she was going to say something, but then just shook her head.

"Well then, just fuck it," Leslie said, "it's none of my business, but your mother spoke to the pastor down there—Henriquez—told him what had happened and asked him—if you must know, got down on her damn knees and begged him—to come up here and speak to Jed. Bought him a plane ticket. And that, as they say, was all she wrote."

"Is that true, Mother?" asked Alyssa, sounding angry all over again, her eyes flooded.

Marion looked over at her beautiful, injured daughter: "Guilty. Sweetheart, I don't know why, but I was waiting for Pastor Henriquez to come by—" she gestured at an empty chair at the end of the table, "so he could tell you himself. But I guess he must have decided to skip the celebration." She glanced back at the glass entry, perhaps expecting some grand moment, and then smiled weakly at what remained of her once large and perfect family.

The next morning, a glorious winter sunrise over the Highland Hills, Marion and Leslie left the Super 8, picked up some coffee and bagels at the Multigrain Cafe, and drove over to the Reformed Church on Huguenot Street. Pastor Henriquez was waiting for them, bundled up in mismatched mittens, boots, ski pants, a fat down parka and a thick sheepskin hat with ear flaps, his round brown face and black eyes the only evidence that a person was hiding inside all that material.

Leslie screamed in delight at his ridiculous getup and then jumped out of the passenger seat, ushered the old man in, shut the door behind him, and slid into the backseat. The seat belt buzzer went off as soon as Marion started off toward Main Street, but the Pastor was too bundled up to reach the belt. Leslie pulled it out from the backseat, but after several awkward tries, he just couldn't bring it across his body and into the latch.

So they drove out to Main Street, made a right and crossed the bridge over the flats toward the mountain, the buzzer beeping at them every two seconds.

The cliffs along the Minnewaska ridge were sparkling pink and gold as they drove wordlessly up the mountain road, buzzer still beeping, slowing around the hairpin turn, the snowy valley below, and then onward to Clove Road, following the fast flowing Peterskill into the small empty gravel parking lot. "A blessed relief!" Leslie muttered to herself when Marion cut the engine and the buzzing finally stopped.

Alyssa's Volvo station wagon was already there, Haley and Travis all bundled up and sitting on the warm hood, waving and smiling. Sam pulled in moments later in a minivan. He got out before Glenda and Aaron had even unbuckled themselves, striding over to Pastor Henriquez and enthusiastically shaking his mitten, thanking him again and again for helping his sister. And for agreeing to conduct the impromptu memorial service at Split Rock, "My dad's favorite place in all of Elting. He told us it was sacred."

Sam looked around then. "Where is Beryl?" He reached into his pocket and pulled out his cell phone, first checking for messages—there were none—and then pushing speed dial #5 just when Stephen skidded the rental car into the shale parking lot. Beryl held up the phone and scowled at her brother.

Despite the Pastor's appearance, it was an unusually warm February day, the kids' coats open as they raced along the gravel path to the bridge over the stream, everyone's hats back in the cars, the rushing of the water growing bolder and more present as they reached the waterfall through the rocks.

As the adults walked solemnly up the path, Sam clutched the small urn he had transported from Costa Rica back to Elting, the one he had placed on the altar at the Dutch Reformed Church, beside a poster-sized picture of Robert standing pensively alone on the wooden bridge at Split Rock, a burst of red and gold autumn leaves in the background.

After a brief eulogy at the Dutch Reformed Church by Pastor Schmidt, who hardly knew anything about Robert, and a request for "anyone who would like to share a remembrance of the deceased to come up and join me here," Robert's friend Garrison had stood up, kissed his invalid wife in the wheelchair next to the bench, and walked up to the lectern. He shook his head and looked down at the assembled family in the front row, Sam and his wife and children, Alyssa and her children, and said, "I am so very sorry."

For a moment it looked as if he was having a stroke himself, his mouth open and nothing coming out, but then he started to talk, first too softly, the packed congregation leaning forward to hear, and then louder, more the voice of the English professor, telling stories, funny stories, of their lives together as boys, as college men, everyone laughing with relief, with renewed—or new—affection for a man so few of them really liked, after all.

Alyssa spoke as well, telling the congregation a little bit about her father's "odyssey" after leaving Elting, how he went on the great journey down south through the Blue Ridge Mountains, New Orleans, Mexico City, Oaxaca, leaving out all mention of Clover, Mountain Eagle, Jen Magruder, "...a man who spent his whole life helping others find themselves, spending his last remaining days on earth trying to find himself, his place on this planet." She broke down when she talked about the ride she took with him from Mexico City to Oaxaca; and she had to stop, gasping for breath, "...and then his heart just gave out."

Sam had to help her down off the podium, back to the bench with his wife and her little girls.

Sam himself had planned—written out on 3 x 5 index cards—a story about a bicycle trip he and his dad had taken from Boston to Provincetown when he was 12, but before he had turned the first card he was already blubbering, holding up his hand and apologizing for not being able to go on.

The minister stood and told the congregation that the spreading of the ashes would be private, but they were all invited back to Sam's home at 242 Woodland Drive to share their memories of Robert, "...now safe and sound in the loving arms of Jesus Christ for eternity."

As they all stood now on the wooden bridge, Marion began by saying she had asked Pastor Henriquez to "officiate" at this unofficial funeral because he was singularly responsible for all of them being able to be together at her Robert's "...most sacred spot on this earth." She smiled a little sadly then, adding "Before all this, everything that happened over the last few years, he used to tell me that there was another even more sacred spot."

Sam winced.

Beryl laughed out loud.

With the endless roar of the relentless rushing water splitting the rock behind him, Pastor Henriquez, bundled in skins, feathers, and his own earthy insulation from the elements, dispensed with the anticipated opening jokes about the weather as well as all liturgical formalities, including the reading of the 23rd Psalm, and began by speaking, not to anyone in particular, but right into the fast rushing stream, thick lips moving in the middle of that round brown face, telling them how the great Bob Marley once said, "Bob Marley isn't my name. I don't even know my name yet."

Then he looked at each member of the family, one by one, tall and short, a two-year-old on Alyssa's hip, standing close together in a half-circle on that wooden bridge, all of them leaning into each other against the cool wind, the cold shadows, the stark reason they were all there, their eyes sparkling with roiling water flowing down the split between the great slabs of rock. The Pastor waited until each member of the family, even the toddler, looked him in the eye, then moved on to the next one.

And when everyone was touched, stopped in time, he sounded

almost angry: "How many of you think you know your name?" He scanned the confused circle, everyone lowering their eyes except five-year-old Travis who raised his hand with a shy smile. Alyssa gently took the child's hand in hers and brought it to her lips. "Just wait a minute, sweetheart," she whispered.

"That's right, child," Henriquez said, softer now. "Of course you know your name. It's the rest of us who are still trying to figure out who we are." He smiled broadly and everyone around the semi-circle smiled with him, relieved that he wasn't going to scold them.

But then his voice grew gravelly again, "This is no garden party, folks, we have more important business than feeling good about ourselves." The smiles disappeared. He scanned the group again. This time there was no need to wait for eye contact. They were all in his power. "We have more important business than showering our petty grief over that gash in the rocks behind me. We have more important business than offering up comforting platitudes about one man's eternal resting place. We have to find out—here, now, and hereafter—how to stop making sense of all this nonsense, how to move ahead, ahead of the fast moving stream behind me.

"I would guess that none of you—none of you—know that I knew the man you know as Robert Tevis. In fact, although I only knew him for a short time, I knew him quite well. I knew his sorrows. I knew his pain. Above all I knew his confusion, his anger, his fear."

He paused then, took off his mittens and dug in the pocket of the fluffy down parka. He took out a handkerchief and blew his nose. "But, you see, I did not know his name." He looked around again. "And you might think, that this Robert Tevis knew who I was, but he did not know my name either. In fact, he did not know that I am a servant of the Lord Jesus Christ. We never spoke of such things. But, trust me…trust me, he also knew my confusion, my anger, my fear.

"Most days we sat on a bench overlooking the beach at Manuel Antonio, two old and crippled men sitting like many old and crippled men on benches. Most days we never spoke to each other, and when we did it was merely to point out a rare white-crowned parrot or just a beautiful green heron. And we smiled sometimes at the funny-looking rasta men with knapsacks full of 'genuine Costa Rican pottery' stumbling down the uneven sidewalk toward the tourists on the beach. But I knew that man like I knew my own soul; and each afternoon I looked forward to sitting in communion with him on that bench. And if he wasn't there, I was sorely disappointed, a day lost.

"One afternoon he joined me later than usual. In fact, I was about to walk back to the church, when he sat down and handed me a folded piece of paper ripped out of one of those spiral notebooks. It said, 'The secret of forgiving everything is to understand nothing. George Bernard Shaw.'"

Beryl gasped out loud then and tears flowed in streams down her cheeks. Stephen, mistaking her anguish, pulled her closer into his chest with his strong hands, but she shook her head and freed herself. Standing alone then, she took a thin, rolled spiral notebook from the pocket of her coat, so thin there could only be a few sheets of paper left clinging to the wire spirals, and she held it up for everyone to see. Then held it flat to her breast.

The Pastor smiled, waited.

She wiped her tears and began: "Jen Magruder and I found this when we cleaned up his cottage. There were just these two pages left in the whole notebook. One with that quote on it and the other that said" —she began to wail—"that he was sorry that he was such a bad father and" —Alyssa turned away, sobbing into Stephen's chest, and Marion leaned her head onto Leslie's shoulder.

Sam stood ramrod straight, no expression on his face. "What else did he write, Beryl?"

She shook her hand through the air as if to blow back the sorrow. "He said that if he died…he said, he said that everything was still as it was in his Will, but that Clover and Mountain Eagle were to get the Winnebago."—She smiled then and, looking at her mother, her voice a whisper above the roaring stream, "Jen Magruder should have the cottage."

"That's it?" Sam said, his lower lip trembling. "That's it?"

Beryl nodded. "I already gave a copy of this to the lawyer." Sam held out his gloved hands as if beseeching the universe for answers.

The Pastor nodded at Beryl. Then he took out another piece of paper from his pocket, a thick piece of paper with straight edges all around. "We have nothing," he said, "unless we have forgiveness." Once again he looked all around the group, now beginning to shiver. "That is the challenge of the living." He held up his hand. "Now I have a few words from your former pastor, Jed Blackstone."

"Don't you dare," Marion whispered, pointing a finger. Sam stepped forward then, perhaps to snatch the paper out of the smaller man's grip, but the Pastor held up his free hand, white palm, brown fingers, and Sam stopped.

And with his palm still up facing the small congregation, Pastor Henriquez scanned each of the faces, cleared his throat and said, "'I am sorry,' he writes. 'Please forgive me.'"

He looked around one more time, knitted anger on all the adults' brows, cold and hunger behind the children's eyes, and began to fold and rip Jed Blackstone's handwritten note, once, twice, three, four, five, six times, and tossed the scraps over the side of the bridge into the wind, white flashes swallowed in the foamy water disappearing over the edge of the rocks into the narrow pool below.

Next he looked at Sam and asked for the urn.

Sam shook his head angrily and walked across the bridge to the rail. "I think I'll take care of this part of the ceremony."

"As you wish," the Pastor said and stepped aside, walking off the bridge and back toward the parking lot, stopping at the wooden information kiosk, and turning to watch from the gravel path.

Holding the urn with both hands, Sam placed it on the wooden rail and removed the top, wisps of sooty ash drifting up and out of the ceramic jug. "I am Sam, Sam I am," he said, looking straight at the Pastor, then turning to his family and biting his upper lip. "Frankly, I was afraid that I wouldn't be able to say anything without breaking down." His eyes were glazed and he nodded to no one in particular. Alyssa, who was now sitting Indian-style on the cold bridge planks, smiled. So did Beryl.

"So I wrote down a few sentences to help myself," he said, twisting his thick torso, and by reaching into his overcoat's breast pocket. his elbow clipped the urn; the urn tipping backward off the rail, the cap falling off as it dropped, bouncing on the rocks, flipping up in shards, wisps of ashen smoke lifting up into the air, drifting into the naked trees, wet ash and bone washing over the falls, disappearing into the cold foam down below.